OLD GOLD

Text copyright ©2012 by Jay Stringer
Printed in the United States of America.

Lyrics from "The Ballad of Hollis Wadsworth Mason, Jr." by Franz Nicolay (c. 2009 Eggshell Armor Music, ASCAP), used with permission.

Published by Thomas & Mercer
P.O. Box 400818
Las Vegas, NV 89140

ISBN-13: 9781612183381
ISBN-10: 1612183387

OLD GOLD

JAY STRINGER

THOMAS & MERCER

"If the choice is cynicism, rage, or giving in;
Which world would you rather live in?"

—Franz Nicolay

My second body this week.
He'd still be alive if I hadn't gone looking for him.
How did it get to this?

ONE

I'd spent two days looking for Lee Owen.

I found him hiding in a council flat on Mount Pleasant. After I followed him home, I headed to The Robin, a grungy local music venue just across the road. There was no cover charge, so I slipped inside and used the pay phone to call my boss. For a minute I stood there, listening to some local band murder an eighties power ballad. When they got to the guitar solo, I stepped back out into the chilly night air. My boss's car was already pulling to the curb. I'm not good with cars. I can't really tell you the makes or models. This one was dark blue, and it looked expensive. Gav Mann was behind the wheel.

"Is he in there?"

That was how Gav greeted me as I slid in next to him, no pretense at friendly banter or introductions. He's a real charmer. He's not the biggest or strongest man in town, but he is one of the most feared. And Owen was the idiot who had stolen from him. The youngest son of Indian immigrants, Gav looked like a businessman who'd come up the hard way. He was always dressed in nice suits, but his hands and knuckles were hard, and his eyes made me think of a tiger. His belly hadn't given way to fat yet, but it looked like it wanted to.

The car smelled of cigarette smoke and air freshener; the smell clung to the seats and closed in around me. There was a small khanda hanging from the rearview mirror. It's the symbol of the Sikh religion, meant to represent independence and spirituality, but when I was with Gav I only noticed the swords.

"Over there, the blue door," I said. "You were quick. Business close by?"

Gav didn't answer me; he just drummed his fingers on the steering wheel.

"It's a dump," he said. "Man steals my money, he can afford better than this."

"He's in hiding," I said. "This is a place nobody would think to look for him."

"Nobody but you," he said.

I shrugged. I'm good at finding people.

"He have the money with him?"

"As far as I know. He's probably planning to rabbit in a couple of days. He thinks he's doing OK."

"Any idea how much he's spent?"

"Not much. He's too clever to splash the cash when everybody's going to be on the lookout for it."

"But not clever enough to leave town. I can't believe he's still here," he said. "If you stole from me, what's the first thing you'd do?"

"Buy a gun."

"OK. But the second? I'm betting you'd get as far away as possible. You wouldn't wait in some shitty council flop five minutes down the road."

I looked down at my feet. There was a dark stain in the upholstery, and I tried not to think about what it could be.

"What are you going to do with him?"

Gav counted out five hundred pounds in fifty-pound notes.

"I don't pay you to think about that, Gyp," he said.

I nodded and took the money. He paid me for a lot of things, but mostly to forget. Gav dialed a number into his mobile and started a call. I let myself out of the car and banged on the roof.

I headed back into town, armed with a chip on my shoulder and some cash in my pocket. There were a select few people who I let call me Gyp or Gypo, and I knew the only reason I let Gav do it was fear. Until just over a year before, I'd been in the police force, and even then many people had seen *Gypsy* before they saw *cop*. There are some things you can never escape.

I pushed in through the door at Posada and up to the bar. It's not the most popular pub in town. It's small and easy to overlook, but some nights it's close to perfect. As the other pubs had given over to trends and buyouts, Posada had remained untouched. It still looked dark and uninviting, it was still cramped, and the menu wasn't painted on the walls in pastel colors. Sometimes it felt like the most welcoming place on earth.

I saw Mary for the first time when she pushed past me into a space at the bar. It must have started to rain outside because her coat was wet. She caught the eye of the barman and ordered straight vodka. Her drink came with ice in it and she frowned. She sipped at it for a moment before making eye contact with me. It was only a second, holding my gaze before looking away. Attitude hooks me before looks, but she had just enough of both. I finished my drink at the same time she finished her second, and I ordered one for each of us. She looked at me again, and her green eyes held me just long enough to pull me forward a few inches. She looked back down at her drink and smiled, bittersweet and wounded.

"My name's Eoin." I leaned in close enough to be heard above the crowd. "Eoin Miller."

"OK."

Her tone said that the conversation was dead. She blew a stray curl of auburn hair out of her eyes, fixed her gaze into the bottom of the glass, and took another sip. I took the hint and left her to it. I talked to the regular faces at the bar for a while. The language of the pub: Music. Films. Football. I coasted through the small talk with a smile, keeping tabs on the woman at the bar as she worked through a hard thirst. It was twenty minutes before closing time when she told me her name.

"Mary," she said. "You were going to ask my name. It's Mary." There was just enough of an Irish flick to her words to make them sound lyrical. "Someone is trying to kill me."

That just about sealed it.

TWO

The staff at Posada always gave me a lot of slack.

When I'd been on the force, my credentials alone had kept trouble from the bar. My new line of work was just as effective, if not more so. I had often been allowed to sit in the back room after hours, with a selection of friends, and drink away the morning.

Of course it wasn't always friends I invited to stay. It could be anybody really. It could, for instance, be a drunken Irishwoman who thought someone was out to kill her.

So with the pub locked it was just the two of us. Mary was an impressive drunk, a different class of drinker. She never lost her composure or showed anything much in the way of emotion. She sat comfortably in the booth in the small back room and smiled occasionally out of the corner of her mouth while blowing that stray hair up out of her face. She didn't slur her words, and she wasn't flirty. She became steadily more intense as the night wore on. Her head tilted to one side when she looked up at me, reminding me of Lauren Bacall.

Her taste in drink never wavered. She stayed with the open bottle of vodka placed on the table between us.

"You're in trouble, then?" It seemed the best place to start.

"Yes."

I could tell she had more to say. Worse, I wanted to ask.

"It sounds complicated."

"Not really," she said, then finally opened up. "My boy-friend—my ex-boyfriend—well, we had an argument."

"Lovers' tiff?"

Her lip curled. "I guess so. It got serious, and he kicked me out. Threw all my stuff into the street."

"Really, where is it now?"

"Still in the street, probably."

I wished I could stop asking questions. But I suppose deep down I hate a mystery.

"Well, it was...it's complicated. See, he thought that I owed him."

"Money?"

She hesitated. "Yeah."

It was a lie, and we both knew it. There was something else there. One thing I had learned in the force is that if you keep asking the same question, one of the answers you get will be the truth. The skill is knowing when that happens. If her boyfriend had really wanted to kill her, he could have done it while he was kicking her out. But it was difficult finding a tactful way to explain that.

I gave it my best shot.

"Look, if he really wanted to kill you, he'd have done it while he was kicking you out."

"He's always making threats, like he'll kick me out or he'll hit me or something. I can tell when he's bullshitting, but this time he sounded serious."

"You let him threaten you?"

She gave me that Bacall look again, and somehow every-thing I'd said seemed foolish.

"Do I look like I'd let someone actually hit me?"

She didn't.

"I see. So this guy thinks you stole something, and he's kicked you out for it and threatened to kill you. Crap boyfriend, if you ask me."

"What are you, an agony aunt?"

I liked her sense of humor; it showed me no respect at all.

"No, just opinionated. Wish I'd thought of that, though. That would have really pissed off my dad."

"And that's how you make your career choices?"

"Is there any other way?"

She laughed again, then poured herself a drink from the bottle. She hadn't touched it for a while now. Things were slowing down. "So what are you working at these days?"

I cleared my throat. I nodded a couple of times, doing that awkward bobbing that men do when they don't know how to explain something. I didn't like to say out loud that I was working for the Mann brothers.

"I do favors, find people, things, you know? I'm saving up to move away, follow my blood."

"Your blood?"

"My dad is Romani. You know"—I paused before saying it—"a Gypsy?"

She blew the hair out of her eyes again, then looked me over again, seeing me in a different way, noticing now my darker features. I can pass for white, but I can also pass for everything else between England and India.

"Yeah, exactly. I'm one of those people who scare the shit out of councils and neighborhood watch schemes. Well, half of me is. My mom was *a Gorjer*—a settled person."

"Aren't Gypsies Irish? I mean that's what they all are on TV, those programs with the big weddings and all that. I always feel like the shows are making fun of my accent."

"No, they aren't Gypsies. We're a whole other thing."

I stopped dead. I hadn't realized just how much I'd opened up here. It was time to pull things back around.

"So this thing that he thinks you stole—"

"The money?"

"The money, whatever it is, a Russian doll for all I care—"

"OK." She nodded. "Whatever it is."

"He's willing to kill you for it?"

She didn't say yes, but I could see the direct look in her eyes and read the word at the back of her throat. Did I want the truth? Yes. But I was drunk and tired, and I wanted a kiss even more.

"Want to come back to my place?"

"Sure."

She said it too quick. She'd known the question was coming. There's always the rational part of my brain that wonders why a woman would go home with me, but there's also the male part that thinks I look like Sam Rockwell. That part shouts loudest.

We walked back to my house, both feeling the loosening effects of the alcohol even more once we got out into the autumn air, stretching a five-minute walk out to fifteen. My house was too big for me. I'd taken on the mortgage in what felt like a previous life, when I was married and pretending to be happy. I'd told my wife I liked it because of its location opposite a public park and because it was big enough to start a family. I'd told my friends I liked it because it was only two streets over from Molineux, and I'd never have to miss a Wolves game again.

This was back when I cared about things like that, when the world mattered to me. Now the house was just a building that was too big for me to heat and too quiet for me to think.

We both paused for a second before I put the key in the door. I hesitated like a schoolboy, and she laughed. She slipped her hand underneath mine over the key, replacing my grip with her own, and turned the key. She stepped into the dark hallway and turned back to me with her bittersweet grin.

"Would you like to come in?"

She was smiling, teasing, which seemed like a good opening. I stepped inside and leaned in for a kiss, but she sidestepped it with a playful smirk and turned to look around. She stooped after kicking something and came back up with a pile of white envelopes, all identical, all addressed to me, and carrying the same post mark.

"Ignoring someone?"

"Just my doctor."

I took the letters from her and dropped them back on the floor before waving for her to look around. There's not a lot of stuff in my house, no unnecessary furniture, no books that I've never read or music that I've never listened to, no food that I don't eat. My wife had never allowed any posters on the walls; she liked them bare and painted. The minute she moved out, I covered those pastel colors with film and concert posters.

Punk rock and seventies cinema are the last revenge of the failed husband.

The only part of the house that had always felt like mine was the kitchen. Cooking was one of the few things I still found any pleasure in. Both of my parents had been good cooks. My mother was a domestic encyclopedia, able to make any meal I challenged her with. My father was a mad genius, combining any variety of herbs and spices with recipes he claimed were passed down through his family. They were never more of a couple than when they were together in the kitchen, laughing and teasing each other as they experimented with food. I had a cupboard dedicated to my father's spices, and in my lowest moments I locked myself away in the kitchen and cooked, throwing in ingredients until I'd invented something new.

Mary was standing in my living room, looking through the CDs, when I brought in the open bottle of wine from the kitchen.

"You're one of *them,* aren't you," she said. "Men in their thirties who manage to ignore popular music and obsess over people who can't sing."

"You've never heard of any of them, then?"

"I didn't say that. I dated a musician once, back in Dublin. He didn't think a band was any good unless they'd had a career of failure and sang about whiskey."

"Sounds like my kind of guy."

"He left me to come over to London and find fame and glory in his own band."

"What happened?"

"I don't know. I assume he failed and sang about whiskey."

I handed her a full glass of wine and retreated to lean against the doorframe. She seemed like she needed space. She frowned again, but it was barely noticeable this time. She sat on the sofa with one of my Tom Waits CDs. She was staring at the cover and seemed lost in memories for a moment.

"We went to see him play in London once. Cost a bloody fortune, and we got lost afterward. Spent two hours walking the city looking for our hotel." She snapped out of it and peered at me. "So there's no girlfriend or wife hiding in any of these rooms?"

I almost coughed into my glass. That was a bit of a jump, but I had known the question would come.

"No, not these days."

"What was it, a girlfriend or a wife?"

"Wife. We're still married, but we haven't been a couple for quite a while."

I didn't know anything about this woman, I realized.

Well, that wasn't true. I knew her name and that she was single. I also knew she liked to drink. I knew she thought someone wanted to kill her. All told, that was more than most first dates, but not enough to shake the apprehension I was feeling. That rational part of my brain was fighting back again, asking why I had a strange woman in my house when she'd said someone was trying to kill her. Then I watched her wiggle to correct her skirt over her legs, the material stretching a little between her thighs, and I decided the rational part of me could shut the hell up.

She stood up and walked over to lean opposite me against the doorframe. She was close enough that I could smell her perfume.

"It didn't feel like stealing at the time." She tilted her head up, like she was looking for approval. "I mean, I'd thought about it for quite a while. You can rationalize anything if you try hard enough, especially after the economy took a shit on us."

She took a sip of wine. The green of her eyes looked darker than it had in the pub, as if great clouds had rolled in. "I just kept thinking I just need one lucky break. One push to get me out of the life I'd been living. I knew how to live the way I wanted, but I just couldn't get there on my own. If everyone could just look the other way, just once."

I kissed her. I'm stupid like that.

I don't remember either of us moving from the door, but soon we had both stumbled up the stairs and into my bed. I made the run to the bathroom for a condom and stood fighting with the wrapper, trying not to think of cold things or waterfalls. By the time I got back into bed she was snoring. It was a soft snore, very cute. I kissed her on the forehead and covered her with the sheets.

I pulled my jeans back on and trod carefully down the stairs, ignoring the noisy step and steadying myself on the banister to stop the world spinning around me. I dropped onto the sofa, and as I closed my eyes, I could feel the booze taking me under.

I stirred for a moment, not knowing if my eyes had been closed for seconds or hours. The thought of making a coffee crossed my mind, but then the sleep came again like a blanket. It wasn't until sun hit my face that I woke up again, daylight streaming in through curtains I'd forgotten to close.

I sat up slowly, squinting against the light and feeling my head throb. As far as hangovers went, this wasn't pretty, but it wasn't the worst I'd had. It felt more like a rugby match than an all-out war. I climbed the stairs and leaned into my room. Mary was almost as I'd left her. Lying in the bed, wrapped in the sheets.

Almost the same.

Except she was dead.

THREE

Don't panic.

Don't panic. Hold it in, concentrate.

Fuck it.

Panic.

I was wrong. I had to be.

I touched her skin and it was cool. It felt like a waxwork model. I felt for a pulse at her wrist. When I couldn't find one I tried for a heartbeat. I brushed her cheek with my hand, hoping for some kind of reaction or a flutter of her eyelids. Anything.

She'd been dead for a few hours, and the realization connected somewhere between my head and my gut. I felt empty, as if someone had pulled a plug in my stomach.

She was wearing her underwear. The rest of her clothes were still piled on the floor where we had left them. There were needle marks on the inside of her right arm. I hadn't pegged her as a junkie, but she could well have shot up after I fell asleep. Or someone may have done it for her. The second option was more likely, because I tore through her pile of clothes but didn't find any drugs or needles.

That wasn't what killed her, though.

I could see marks around her neck, a thick band of skin that was raised and swollen where something had squeezed.

One of my old work ties was on the floor with her clothes, and it hadn't been there the night before.

I'd always hated wearing a tie, but I'd never hated the sight of one as much as I did right then. I noticed a tattoo of a butterfly on her inner thigh, and right then it looked like the saddest thing I'd ever seen. I stared at it for a moment, transfixed.

Then I felt the panic build inside, running up my spine and taking over as my knees began to shake. I made it to the bathroom just in time to throw up.

I stood up when I finished retching, feeling light-headed. I splashed my face with cold water, pressing my fingers into my eye sockets, as if I could erase the image of her dead body. I tried to stop breathing so fast. Now was the time to think clearly. Slow down. Do the sensible thing.

But I didn't move to pick up the phone. Instead my father's voice ran around my head.

"If there's trouble, be far away from it. If you can't be far away, run like hell."

I seemed to feel his hand on my shoulder when I thought of that speech. I could picture him, face and arms covered with marks from police beatings, for being the wrong race in the wrong place.

"They'll just see a Gypsy, they won't ask questions, won't stop to see who else might have done it. They will kick the shit out of you and lock you up. If your hands are out of sight, they'll assume you've got a knife. Whatever happens out there is not your concern. Run."

Born to run.

This is where I really fucked up. I shouldn't have listened to my dad's voice in my head. But I couldn't help it. I ran downstairs, pulled on my jacket, grabbed my keys, and fled.

I drove. I didn't have a plan, and I didn't need one. My mind had gotten good at autopilot over the past year, and a familiar fog drifted in over my thoughts, a white blanket wrapped around the inside of my skull. I tried listening to music, but I couldn't settle in, nothing would distract me. If I'd driven south I would have hit town after town, the epic urban sprawl that leads to Birmingham. Instead I drove west, where the city gives way to wide-open country and to the sleepy market towns that separate England from Wales. There was a buzz at the base of my skull, like tinnitus in the wrong place, something I could feel rather than hear. A few times on the force I'd witnessed violence, and this was the same reaction I'd had, a distance growing between me and the world.

The buzz didn't begin to fade, the blanket to let go of my brain, until I reached Bridgenorth. An ancient town built on the ruins of a castle that had been sacked after the civil war, it always looked to me like an island of rock surrounded by countryside. It had always been the perfect place to think. It would also be the perfect place to defend against a Welsh invasion, but that didn't seem likely. I was sitting in the beer garden of a pub I liked, with a pint of bitter in one hand and a cigarette in the other.

And I don't smoke.

Every time I closed my eyes, I saw Mary's dead body. I kept trying to think of her as just a woman, someone I was detached from, the way they had taught me on the force. "No place for crusades or grudges," the advice went. "Don't get attached." But each time I started to build up a wall against Mary, she would break it down with her smile or with that lock of hair she was always blowing out of her face.

I gave up trying to forget her and thought of calling the police. But I was screwed if I did that. I was just a dirty

Gypsy with a corpse on my hands. She was strangled in my bed. With my tie. Her prints were all over my house. Everybody in the city knew I was dirty, and the police wouldn't trust me to boil an egg. As my dad used to say, there would be no questions, no pause.

My other option was to call the Mann brothers. They'd paid off the mortgage on my house. The jobs they paid me for kept me in food and drink. All that was left was the formality of handing them my soul, which is what I'd be doing if I asked them to clean this up.

Either way, I was trapped.

I left the pint on the table and stubbed out the cigarette, suddenly feeling the taste of it in my mouth. I found my car in the street outside and drove back home, listening to some bland soul station on the radio. It was like driving forward in time as the market town and Roman roads slowly dropped away and the tarmac and factories appeared, signs of the industrial age kicking in. As I neared the city, the industrial age gave way to the bankrupt age and the views were of a region whose identity had been snatched away. It had been a long time since these factories had stopped pumping soot and smoke into the sky, but the clouds always seemed to hang a little lower and darker over the area.

There wasn't much traffic as I neared Wolverhampton, as if the whole world was in the same daze I was. I killed the engine after pulling into my driveway and stared up at the windows of my house. I didn't want to move, either forward or back. I wanted to close my eyes and stay right where I was, forever.

I breathed in and out, willing the hole in my gut to close, and got out of the car. I unlocked the front door and pushed it open, stepping into the house before I had time to change my mind.

It felt wrong.

Even with a corpse in my bed this morning, the house had still felt as if it had life in it, as if there were more people in it than just me. This time, though, the emptiness and still-ness clung to my hallway.

I climbed the stairs slowly, taking them one at a time with heavy feet. I reached the top and stepped into my bedroom.

It was empty.

Mary was gone.

My bed was stripped bare; the sheets had vanished along with her body, her clothes, and my tie. I felt the buzzing at the base of my skull again as I wandered from room to room, trying to find where the corpse had walked to.

I tried to imagine everything was different. That I'd been wrong. That Mary wasn't dead. That she'd woken up, cleaned the room, and left. That I was free and clear and a silly little boy.

Yeah, right.

Someone had moved the body. Someone had cleaned my room, removed the evidence, and taken the murder weapon with them. Who would do that? Someone was fucking with me, and I had no idea what the hell I'd stumbled into.

I closed my eyes and tried the opposite trick now, tried picturing what made her human again in my mind, the smile, the hair, her tattoo. But all I could see was her dead body.

FOUR

I sat at the kitchen table, looking around my space. It felt like someone else's house now. It had never felt completely mine. Even when we bought it, it had felt more like Laura's project. She was always talking of grand plans. Of a nursery in the front bedroom, of a music room for me where I could put up big speakers and tune out, of a desk for her in a space that would be her own. That was another year and another life. Now the house was just the scene of a woman's murder.

Somewhere out there was a killer and a dead body. Someone had gone to the trouble of killing Mary in my home, then removing her. But they'd also taken my tie, which incriminated me. It was like a joke with the punch line missing. Every instinct I had still told me to get the hell out of Dodge.

To give in to my blood.

I owned the house outright—I could simply walk away if I wanted. Packing wouldn't be hard. In truth I'd never fully unpacked. I had clothes in my bedroom and food in the kitchen. In the living room I had CDs, DVDs, and the equipment to play them on. In a cupboard I had a box of my wife's things, not a lot, just the things she'd left behind.

But what would that achieve? I wouldn't be able to just forget Mary. She kept speaking to me. Fragments of conversation from last night kept drifting to the front of my mind. If she'd died in someone else's house, it would have meant nothing to me. But she was a lost woman who couldn't find a better soul than mine to cling to on her last night on earth.

Fuck it.

Somebody out there had something on me, and I knew it. They were dangling the threat of the corpse over me. Stay quiet, and it could stay vanished. Leaving town would be OK too, as long as I kept my mouth shut. Poke around, start asking questions, and it could reappear. Whoever was holding Mary's body was counting on my silence, thinking that the threat of a murder rap would scare me. Well, they were right. But I was also stubborn, stupid, and angry. I hate secrets. I hate mysteries. And I hate being used.

I thought again about the needle mark in Mary's arm. Drugs. It had to be drugs. Someone had shot her up last night, and there would be no other reason to do that. Someone was making a point. If it involved drugs, then somebody in town would have heard about it. These things never stay secret. The drug trade is like any other, full of office politics and juicy gossip. All you need to do is find the right office junior and apply pressure.

I'd ask around and maybe I'd get lucky.

Maybe I'd get killed.

FIVE

In this line of work, you're only as good as the people you lean on for information.

I was going to have to start at the bottom.

If you really want to see the drug trade at work, you head out to the council estates and the parks or take a walk around the high-rise flats or boarded-up houses. That's where you see capitalism at its youngest and purest. If the brains of these kids were put to military use, we would never lose a war.

The dealers you find in the city center are the ones on the edge of the wheel. They're amateurs and losers with big talk and short attention spans. They taste their own gear and are on first-name terms with the police who roust them. You don't tap these guys up if you want to know where the money is, but they are useful. If you want to find someone higher up the tree, you pull all the branches you can reach. My approach is simple: piss off as many people as I can until I get to the right guy.

Matt was always the first person I'd check with and the last person you'd buy anything off. He hung around Saint Peter's Church, sitting by the fountain or in the grounds of the church itself. He was a rodent-like kid—small and greasy, wrapped in an old army coat with a German flag on the arm. He used to be a student at the university. After selling skunk to his friends, he realized how much money he could make by selling to other people. As soon as he started peddling his gear outside of campus, he officially became a problem for the university management. That, and his own spiraling habit, had led him to where he was now. Homeless, broke, and more addicted to the stuff he was trying to sell than his customers were.

"Eoin!"

He found me before I found him, running across the churchyard to greet me. Was he limping? Hard to tell. He didn't seem to be supporting his own weight very well. He was thinner than I remembered, and he smelled worse. When he smiled, it was with more gums and less teeth than before.

"Hey, I was just looking for you."

"Me?" He paused and looked round, telegraphing what was going through his head. "What you want to know?"

I could see the hope in his eyes. Here was his shot at being useful again, at being part of something. He was too sensitive, and everyone knew it. His time was marked if he didn't get out of the trade. If I were a nicer man, I'd make a mission of straightening him out. But I already had one junkie for a brother and no interest in adopting another one.

"Just a couple questions. I'll stand you a couple of drinks next time I'm in Posada."

"OK," he sniffed, wiping at his nose. I decided that he looked more like a beat-up old dog than a rodent.

"Anything big happening that I don't know about?"

"Like what?"

"Any heists? Any stashes been nicked?"

"Shit, you know. The usual. Gaines and the Mann brothers have got everything divided up, and nobody touches them, so it's all small shite, school kids who don't know any better."

Ransford Gaines was old money crime: gambling, protection, and vice. He'd expanded into drugs sometime in the eighties, when the Birmingham gangs were encroaching. Since then, he and the Mann brothers had agreed to disagree. "Any new product?"

"Nah. I heard that Claire Gaines was into meth, the wrong way, and her old man was going to start cutting the supply and keep her clean, but nothing's new."

Claire was the youngest Gaines daughter. She was a loose cannon, everybody knew that. "Have there been any new faces?"

"Yeah, some new guy. Polish, I think."

"Selling in town?"

"Yeah, in the pubs and clubs. He's probably going to try and get a place in the estates."

That would be interesting. Once a new person started pushing in on the estates, there would be hell to pay.

"What's this all about anyway? Not like you to be sniffing round drugs."

"Bad joke, Matt, very bad joke. Any dealers having girl trouble?"

"Of course. You know how it is."

I turned to leave. I could think of better ways to waste my time. Most of them involved sitting in Posada. I tried one last question.

"You know an Irish girl name of Mary?"

"No, is she fit?"

I laughed and walked away. I passed through the church gate and headed toward the steps.

"I still get the drinks, right?"

"Whatever, Matt. Yeah."

I'd forgotten about the drinks before I reached the steps.

I headed back out and started tapping up the street dealers. They weren't all as low as Matt. In fact, the majority of them were at least three showers and a meal better off. But it's hard to get anything solid out of a drug addict. I needed someone who didn't use the product. I needed to go higher up the tree.

There was one person who kept eluding me.

I must have asked a dozen people, "You seen Jellyfish lately?"

Everyone had the same answer or variations on it. He wasn't around or he was out of town or he owed them money.

Jellyfish wasn't a dealer, but they all knew him. He was a professional good time. As far as I knew, he'd never held an honest job, but he always knew where the party was, who was doing the fucking, who was being fucked, and who was peddling the best gear. Like an old-school tobacco company rep, he'd always turn up at a party with free samples from whoever was protecting him that month—usually the Mann brothers.

It was usually quicker to get information from him than to go looking for it myself. I'd never known exactly where his nickname came from or what his real name was. I'm sure he started out as a Jeremy or a Justin, something along those lines. The nickname had something to do with him going both ways. Or, to be more precise, he went whichever way the money was.

Another question that kept turning me up blanks was, "Know a girl named Mary?"

"Nah, man, she owe you money?"

"Nah, man, she cut and run on you?"

"Yeah, man, I heard she's your mom."

I was getting nowhere.

I tried a few of the local pubs, telling myself I was still looking for information when really I was just drinking. As I left the last of the pubs, a skinny Asian-looking kid bumped into me. He wore a turban low over his forehead, more like a bandanna, and I saw a kara on his wrist, the metal Sikh bracelet. As he walked away he said, "Bauser wants to see you."

Bauser was a couple of steps up the food chain. He was one of the stoppers for the Mann brothers, and he was rarely away from his estate or one of the pubs on the outskirts of the city. My questions had got me noticed.

I followed the messenger down past a row of kebab shops. He turned into a side street that I recognized as the back entrance to an old rock club. He accelerated to walk away faster, making it clear he'd done his job.

I heard my name called, and Bauser stepped toward me from a doorway.

He had a gun.

SIX

You don't really see guns in the city.

They're expensive, and the bullets are precious.

But they're there.

Never let anyone tell you there isn't a gun culture in the Midlands. They're kept out of sight so that the police don't have to worry about them, and the public can feel safe because the media just wants to talk about knives. But you see them. For example, I was seeing one in Bauser's hand.

I'd talked to armed kids when I was on the force, but my job had provided protection then. Even without an actual badge pinned to my chest, one hovered over me. But I didn't have that protection anymore, and when I saw the silver of the gun sticking out the sleeve of his hoodie, I felt my stomach flex just a little.

"What's up, Bauser?"

I'd known him a long time and watched him grow. I'd arrested him when he was barely into his teens and still going by the name Boz, a kid wanting to play at Scorsese. But now he was growing into his frame, and he knew there weren't many black kids in Scorsese films. His broad shoulders flexed a little, a play at showing me he was a grown-up, but in his cheeks and eyes I could see he was still younger than Matt.

Our streets are run by children.

"You've been asking a lot of questions today."

"Not been getting any answers."

He eyed me for a minute.

"You've been asking about our stuff. You knew it would come up the chain."

"I hoped it would, yes. Baus, I need you to tell me what's going on."

He stepped in close and patted me down. He knew I wouldn't be armed; I'd never carried on the force. If I'd wanted an illegal one after leaving, I would have gone through him. But he went through the motions.

"Ask your questions," he said, once he finished.

"Has anyone had a stash stolen?"

"All the time, man. But you mean a big stash? No."

"I've heard about a new face selling. That mean anything to you?"

"The Polish guy? Yeah. He's selling good shit, good price. He's not really making any moves into serious territory, though."

"Is he going to?"

"How the hell would I know?"

A new face would annoy the establishment. For all the people out there moving and selling the drugs, only a handful of people at the top take the money. And it's an uneasy truce between them as it is.

"Who are you asking for?" Bauser asked.

"Myself."

Bauser eyed me again. His gun hand looked a little twitchy. Not the kind of nervous twitch that filled me with confidence. He would be wondering why I hadn't gone straight to his bosses, the Mann brothers.

"Gyp, you've never been interested in drugs. Why start now?"

On the list of people I allow to call me Gyp, those with guns tend to rank quite highly. I switched up my questions.

"Who's working for this new guy?"

"Say what?"

Everyone's an American these days.

"Look, this new guy's been selling in the city and pubs, right? He can't be doing all of this by himself. If he's not taken any territory yet, he doesn't need a lot of people to stand and make a claim. But he's got to have people out there using their feet, pushing for him."

Bauser blinked a couple of times. He didn't say anything.

He'd always been loyal to the Mann brothers. That had never been in question. But a blink is a blink.

"Baus, are you switching up?"

His body language changed, all wounded pride and anger. Defiance. His words and tone changed as well.

"Fuck you, man, nobody questions my loyalty. I've always been straight."

His eyes told a different story.

So whatever this new guy was, he wasn't stupid. He wasn't trying to take away territory from the Mann brothers or Gaines. He was letting them keep the territory; he was taking the staff.

So he was smart, but was he a killer?

I could imagine the motive. Fucking with me would give him another way to get at the Mann brothers. Or leverage to hire me, if he was still looking for staff.

"OK, Bauser, I'm sorry. Listen, you hear anything interesting, let me know, yeah?"

He nodded and put his hand out for a shake.

Respect is important with these boys; if you don't show it, you don't have it. And if you don't have it, you don't get to speak. I shook his hand. I didn't give him any cash. Mid-level guys never touch cash, and you don't disrespect them by offering bribes. You just make deals, always make it about business.

"Listen, I'm serious. I've got a personal stake in all this right now. Any moves made by this guy, or against him, you tell your uncle Eoin."

He laughed, which was as close as I was going to get to a yes.

We nodded at each other, and I walked back the way I'd come.

I still needed to find Jelly, and I'd just thought of the best place to start.

The Mann brothers' newest investment was a couple of miles out of town, behind the Angel pub on Junction Road, not far from where I'd found Lee Owen. The council had built a new block of low-rise flats and made room for it by clearing away an older estate of almost exactly the same design, relocating the tenants, and smoothing out the land. They should have salted the earth too, because the minute the new blocks went up, some of the old tenants came back.

It had been the perfect plan. The Mann brothers had owned most of the estate and sold it at a good price to the council. After the building work was done, the brothers used a front company to buy the property at a discount through an urban redevelopment scheme. The face-lift had worked, and there were young, honest families in many of the apart-ments, but also in the mix was a collection of stash houses, safe houses, pill presses, and grow ops. But the buildings were kept clean and the paint was fresh, so nobody seemed to mind.

The man given the job of keeping an eye on all of this, making sure the buildings were clean and everything stayed low profile, was Bobby. He wasn't stupid, but his brain worked at a different speed. This gave him a simple, trustworthy air and made him the perfect caretaker for a number of the Mann brothers' estates. It also made people underestimate him, which is why he came in handy when I was investigating things. Just as Jellyfish was the life of every party, Bobby was ignored wherever he went. He could often ask questions that I couldn't, and as we both worked for the same people, I didn't have to pay him for it.

I pressed the intercom buzzer for Bobby's flat and waited. There was no answer.

I took a look around, but the grounds were quiet. There were no kids playing outside, nobody to ask. I tried again, and when I got no answer, I tried the buzzers for other apartments that I knew Bobby looked after.

On the fourth attempt I found him. His voice sounded electronic through the intercom. It was like talking to Stephen Hawking. It sounded like there was someone else with him, making strange noises in the background.

"Hey, Bobby," I said. "Can I come up?"

He didn't reply, but the door buzzed open, and I made my way up to his floor.

As I came out of the stairwell, he stepped out of the first door on the left, pulling the door almost shut behind him. I heard the strange noise again, halfway between a chew and a whimper. I thought it was a dog for a second, but then I heard very human moaning.

"Who you got in there?"

He shrugged. Like I said, he's good at being discreet.

"Whoever it is doesn't sound too healthy."

"Broken jaw," he said. "I'm trying to feed him."

I could make an educated guess about who'd be locked away in a Mann brothers' safe house with a broken jaw. It didn't take much.

"Lee Owen, huh?"

Bobby shrugged again, a great non-answer.

I wasn't surprised that Lee hadn't had the money on him when Gav Mann had paid him a visit last night. They'd be keeping him almost healthy until he gave up the dough.

"Listen, have you seen Jellyfish around?"

Bobby shook his head. "Naw. Last time I spoke to him, he was off chasing some blonde from the university. You know Jelly."

"Could you take a look for him? I really need to catch up with him."

Bobby shrugged again. This time his shoulders rolled forward in a way that said yes.

"Have you heard of any stash grabs lately? Anything big."

He stared at me. I could see his brain working behind his eyes as my question worked its way into his memory and the answer worked its way back out.

"No, not for a while."

"OK. I'm hearing about a Polish dealer? You know anything about him?"

He shook his head. This time the answer hadn't taken as long to retrieve.

The moaning sound came from inside again, and I touched Bobby's shoulder.

"You better get back inside and feed the poor bastard."

As he turned to step back inside, I thought of something. The last thing I needed was to go back to that empty house, to sleep alone with memories and ghosts.

"Hey, Bobby. I might need a place to crash tonight. The house is giving me the creeps. Is there a vacancy?"

He rummaged in his pocket and pulled out a keychain that was so burdened it seemed fit for a jail warden. He selected a copper-colored Yale key and a silver one of a different make. He worked them off the chain and handed them to me.

"Number thirty-four is clean. I repainted it yesterday, so behave. The gold key is for downstairs."

"Cheers, Bob."

He nodded. He stepped back into the flat, and before the door shut, I caught the coppery smell of blood. I pushed the thoughts away. I was carrying enough around without feeling guilty for Lee Owen. He chose his fate when he stole. Then I thought of Mary and how she'd stolen as well.

Too many questions.

I shook my head and left.

SEVEN

I was drained.

My brain was fizzing with images and sparks, altogether too many thoughts that were failing to connect to one another. A headache was building, but my body was too tired to follow through on it.

I'd gone the whole day without food, and as the night set in I decided to do what I always did when I was hungry: I checked in at Posada for a couple of drinks. I settled in at the bar for a while and talked to some of the regulars. Their jokes were as bad as usual, but laughing at them made me feel human again. My wires cooled down. I flicked through the day's paper. Usual crap. The local council was going bankrupt, the police were short staffed. There was a story of a guy in Walsall who'd been lying dead in his council flat for three years before anyone noticed. You couldn't make that shit up.

How could you be dead for three years and nobody notice? Not even a creditor. Dark thoughts, nothing you want floating round your head unchecked.

As I sipped at a pint of mild, not really in the mood to get drunk, a woman slid in next to me at the bar. I kept my eyes on my drink. There was no way on earth I was making the same mistake two nights running.

After a few seconds, though, I could feel her looking at me.

Don't.

    Don't.

"Hello," she said.

Fuck.

Somehow I'd known she was going to talk to me. In hindsight, I should have made the connection there and then, but at the time all I wanted to do was be left alone. I didn't think an all-out glare would be a fair response. Nor did it seem the moment to explain that the last woman I'd chatted to in here was dead.

So I ignored her instead.

"Fine, then." She ordered a glass of Coke and said to the kid behind the bar, "Grumpy here is paying."

For some reason I turned and half smiled at that. Maybe it was the class with which she'd handled the situation, maybe it was just stupidity.

Leaning against the bar she looked to be a few inches shorter than me, maybe around five feet seven, and maybe a year or so older. Her nose had been broken and reset at some point when she was younger, but it suited her, added a little wear and character, which was backed up by the mischievous glint in her eye.

"Oh, now he's interested."

She turned to smile at me, and it took a few years off her age. I revised my guess and put her about five years younger than me—and very attractive once you'd looked at her a couple of times.

And she was a prostitute.

I felt safe in the guess. Sometimes you can just tell.

"I'm broke," I said and returned to my drink.

"And tactful too," she said.

I smiled again. I couldn't help it. I liked this girl, and she seemed to like me.

Of course, liking me was her line of work.

She looked down at the bar and smiled, just a little, like it was a game. Mary had pulled the same look. Like she'd been counting in her head how long it would be before my next move.

But this girl didn't wait for that move.

"Don't know about you," she said. "But I'm tired and worn out. I've had a crap day, and nobody seems interested in me when they can get a younger model. I could do with a cheap laugh."

I held my hand out, and she took it.

I used the keys Bobby had given me to let us into flat number 34. It was modern and tidy and lacked any kind of character. It had a small hallway that opened onto a bedroom, a bathroom, and a living room. The living room had a small kitchen area in an alcove. The walls had just been painted, as Bobby had said, over the plaster. There were marks on the wall in the hallways, dents where something heavy had hit. The whole place smelled too clean, as if someone had worked hard at disinfecting and covering bad odors. I didn't want to think why.

I sat down awkwardly on the sofa and thought, Yes, you're really doing this, and she is really here. "So what do we do now?"

"You need it explained?" She smiled, but there was a sad, distracted look in her eyes that I would have missed if it wasn't part of what was attractive about her.

"Well, no, I just…ah…I'm not used to this."

"Imagine I'm just a girl you picked up in a bar."

"God no, don't go there." I wanted to think about anything but picking up girls at bars. Because that meant thinking about Mary.

"OK. Normal small talk it is. Where do you like to go?"

A smile played across my face as I thought of a list. This was working. I'd spent at least a few minutes already pretending that I hadn't found a dead girl in my house that morning.

"Films," I said. "I love the cinema, but that's never very good for dates because you can't talk. It's not a good thing."

"You think? I always liked the cinema for a first date; it replaced the awkward silences with explosions and maybe even dinosaurs. Then you could talk about the film afterward, and you'd have some kind of common ground to base a conversation on, to break the ice."

"You know, I never thought of it that way before."

"What's your favorite movie?"

"Funny, I have no idea. I mean, I love a lot of movies, but I've never thought of what my all-time favorite would be."

"You strike me as a *French Connection* kind of guy. I bet you love that movie."

"You're not wrong, I do."

"You've got that harried look, like the guy in it, the younger one."

"Roy Scheider," I said. "He was in *Jaws* too."

"You know his name?" She laughed. "He looked different then, though. But in *The French Connection*? Totally looks like you."

That wasn't a look I'd choose, but it was better than Gene Hackman.

I was warming to movie chat now. "Or maybe something really old with one of those old-time actresses in it. Bacall, someone like that."

"Yeah, those are great movies. The women are the only people who ever really know what is going on."

"How about you?"

"I never know what's going on," she said.

"No, what's your favorite movie?"

She closed her eyes and beamed.

"Easy. *Big Trouble in Little China*. It's just so much fun. When Kurt Russell says, 'How'd you get up there,' and the old guy shouts down, 'Wasn't easy.' Makes me laugh every time."

And just like that, we knew each other and we had sex.

And it was good. It was easy and functional, and we both seemed to enjoy it. It was sober sex, something I'm not so used to. We smiled as we went. We didn't make too many mistakes. We didn't overdo the noise or hurry through it. I relaxed into my orgasm, and she let out a contented groan, but then I'm sure she always seemed to enjoy it.

I lay back and thought I might actually sleep, but my stomach wouldn't let me be. It wanted actual food, which was just inconvenient.

"How about I buy us some food and a decent drink?"

"I'd like that," she said.

Before I stood up, I took some cash out of my wallet and left it on the side table for her. I'd never paid a prostitute before and didn't know the polite way to discuss price, but I figured she'd tell me if it wasn't enough.

I shopped at the all-night garage down the road and returned to cook a meal fit for royalty. I assume kings and queens enjoy a fry up as much as the rest of us. I cooked us a plate full of chips, bacon, and beans and my famous scrambled eggs.

I tried to pour her a drink, but all she wanted was coffee, so I made up for it with a large whiskey for myself.

She leaned over the plate and pointed at me with a forkful of egg.

"So what other movies do you like? Anything made since the seventies?"

I had to think about it.

"Well, yeah, there have been a lot of good movies since then, but I guess it's just easier to stick to the old ones, y'know? When you're younger, you've got more time to take in movies and to think them through. But now it's a bonus if you get time to watch one, and they have no relevance to your everyday life."

"True. But that can be a good thing, the escapism of it. Let's face it, neither of us is a secret agent, and neither of us has a spaceship, so it's fun to watch something like that."

She looked at my empty glass. "You got through that quick."

"It's all in the reflexes."

She laughed. As her smile faded, I caught a glimpse of her off guard, with that distant look in her eyes. I always seemed to go for people with a doomed look about them.

The meal earned me a freebie. That or my taste in movies. It was different the second time, colder and meaner. Neither of us had our minds or hearts in the room with us. I kept imagining it was Mary in bed with me, living and breathing.

I must have dozed off then—a mixture of the day's stress and the big meal, not to mention the sex—because I don't remember her leaving.

I woke up on my own. My wallet was still on the bedside table, and she hadn't taken any cash. I decided that made her the most honest person I'd ever known. And I'd never asked her name.

I was thinking about honesty as I drifted back into dreams.

EIGHT

"I'd like to report someone missing."

I was in the reception at the Wolverhampton police station, a large redbrick building in the city center with modern lines and too many windows. It had been my station for a while, near the end.

I'd woken up still thinking about honesty. The police had resources. I'd have a go at reporting Mary as a missing person and fill in a bit of paperwork. The police could well do nothing, but if there was some drug investigation going on that she tied into, alerting them would make more progress than any amount of street walking I could do.

The clerk at the desk wanted to know who I was reporting missing.

"Her name is Mary."

"That's her first name?"

"Yes. I think."

"You think?"

"I'm not exactly sure."

The cop in me was cringing.

If only I'd thought this through. Or thought it through a bit more than I had.

"What relation are you to this missing person?"

"She talked to me in the pub."

"So you're not family?"

"No."

"Not a boyfriend, husband?"

"No."

"A friend?"

"Not really, no."

"And you don't know her name."

"Not getting very far here, am I?"

While I'd been talking, the desk sergeant had taken a form out of a filing cabinet against the far wall. He'd got as far as putting down the date and his name when he started asking me the details, but now he put the form down behind the desk, out of sight.

"How long has she been missing?"

"About a day and a half, two days at the outside."

"So this girl, this woman, you *think* her name is Mary. And she's not related to you or friendly with you in any way. How, exactly, do you know she's missing?"

Because she died in my bed.

"Because I haven't seen her since the pub."

"Had you ever seen her before she turned up at the pub?"

"No."

"And has anyone spoken to you about her since?"

"No."

Well, she has spoken to me a couple of times, but that's just my mind playing tricks.

"Are you willing to put this in writing?"

I shook my head and let my frustration show. I was wasting my time. I didn't know why I'd thought this would be a good idea.

I needed to regroup.

I left the station, blinking in the daylight, and ended up in the darkest, oldest-looking coffee shop I could find.

It looked like a relic from the eighties. Old women behind the counter served you while wearing burgundy aprons, and the selection of cakes looked homemade. If I'd ordered something fancy, like a latte, I'd probably have been met with a blank stare.

I settled in near the window with the day's paper, a filter coffee, and a slice of carrot cake. I scanned the paper, starting on the back page and working toward the front. The front-page news was about a pensioner being handcuffed to a radiator and beaten. She had broken bones in her face and arm, and it was all for her savings of eighty-six pounds. She had given up the money as soon as she was threatened, but the assailant beat her anyway.

A shadow fell across my paper and stayed there, waiting to be acknowledged.

I knew who it was before looking up, as he had a way of sighing when he was waiting me out, the sound of him climbing up to a moral high ground.

"Becker," I said. "Of all the gin joints."

Terry Becker was probably my best friend. He was the only person willing to put up with my shit for any length of time, and I was the only person willing to put up with his attempts at improving himself. He went through phases: foreign cinema, ethnic music, bad food. He went to great lengths to try and be somebody he wasn't.

Which was probably the real reason we got on so well.

He'd also introduced me to my wife, Laura, which was something I'd still not killed him for. He was local CID, out of my old office, and he was either here for a favor or to lecture me. Probably both. He was holding two drinks, a Coke for him and what looked, unfortunately, like a Coke for me too, and he slid in opposite me and pulled my uneaten cake toward him. He sighed again as he sat down, and I noticed the increased bulk that was pushing against his shirt. His cheeks too were a little rounder than they used to be.

"I've been trying to get hold of you. You ignoring my messages?"

"Yes."

I had never got round to telling him that I'd thrown my mobile away. Too many missed calls from friends and family, too many voice messages from Dr. Guthrie.

He sipped from his drink, and I stared at mine.

"How you doing, Eoin?"

That was always the first question he asked me these days, and I had no idea why. I felt a little anger rise, the same burning sensation I got whenever someone used that bland phrase to hide that they were asking about my health. As if it was their business. I shrugged and sipped at my drink.

"Fair enough." He tried again. "I hear you were just round at my place, trying to file a missing persons?"

"You must have heard wrong."

"No, I don't think so. I watched you leave the building."

"I could've sworn I was in bed all morning."

"I swung by your place earlier. You weren't there."

"I didn't say it was *my* bed."

I didn't really want to push this. Becker was my best friend, yes, but he was a cop, and I didn't want him involved in anything that might test our limits.

"So who's the missing person?"

Shit.

"Nobody, really. Your desk officer pointed out to me how silly I was being, the error of my ways. There's a reason I was a lousy pig."

"Now we both know that's not true." He chewed on a forkful of carrot cake, his lips making smacking noises as he ate. "I could help you, you know?"

"No, really, it's nothing."

"Now I'm even more intrigued. A missing person that you don't want me looking into?"

"Leave it, Beck."

I pushed out of my seat and fetched another slice of cake from the counter. I sat back opposite Becker and took half of the slice with one bite. Seeing his empty glass, I slid my Coke across to him.

"Thanks." Becker lifted the drink in a salute.

"What for? You're paying."

"So, OK, anyway. The reason I've been trying to get you is to do you a favor, to throw some work your way."

"Thanks, but I've got a full plate."

"Is it a paying plate?"

I had to concede that one.

"Well, it's funny you should be on a missing person hunt. See, that's why I was so pushy about who you're looking for. The job I've got is the same deal. It's about a missing person, a student."

"Why should I get involved in a case you guys can't even be bothered to carry?"

"It's not that," he said.

"Oh, come on, I know how it works. Let me know when I'm close. A student has gone missing partway through a semester. I'm guessing maybe just before a round of exams?"

"Pretty close."

"So it's *no deal* for you boys. Unless there's any proof of a crime, you're not going to look into it beyond maybe a few token efforts for the family and the local paper. Not when there are all those sexy terrorists to look for."

He laughed. "If only it were that simple, mate. I long for the days when London was shitting itself over everybody with dark skin and a beard. I don't need to tell you how many people round here have dark skin and beards, how much overtime that led to. Glory days, glory days."

"So what is it now?"

"Now it's seeing how much work they can get out of us for almost no pay. No overtime. Pensions cut, hours cut, bonuses frozen. They just don't want to give us any bloody money. Unless there's a riot. Then we have to chase down every kid in a hoodie."

"They get you chasing all that?"

"Biggest police action I've seen since we went on alert after the London bombings, and you know how that was. We kicked in every bloody door in the Midlands, it felt like. Got some actual police work done, arrested people, it felt surreal. You'd have been in on it too if you hadn't dropped out."

"If it was so great, then why not get some more actual police work done and find this kid?"

"Well, see, that's where you come in. The case isn't open. It's not been reported, officially."

Now I was interested. I leaned forward. "What's going on?"

"You remember Michael Perry?"

I did. He'd been a generation ahead of us in the force, working his way up by playing the game the right way. "Chubby guy, glasses? Ambitious, never said anything to offend anybody?"

"That's him. Though he's not so chubby now; he's lost most of it again. His son has gone missing, and he wants it looked into off the books, so to speak."

"Why? He's brass, he can just send the full weight of the force into it; get the kid found in about five minutes."

Becker shook his head and leaned in a bit closer. He gave me that look of his that said, this is top secret. I'd always wondered if he thought that look meant the rest of the world would actually stop listening.

"Perry wants to move into politics. The force is bringing in those new commissioner posts, elected like in America. Looks like Perry wants a run at that and maybe the Labour party after that. So he needs—"

"So he needs this to be kept secret, so that Daddy's big career doesn't get hurt? So if you do it quietly, you guys can still look into it off the books."

"Yes. We have been. I have been, I mean. But it's not going well because people still know I'm a badge. Pretty soon word will get out. You can ask questions we can't. It might only take you a couple of conversations to find him."

"What a tempting offer, I must say. You really sold me on that one."

"OK, don't look at it as a favor to me. Truth be told, I couldn't give a shit. If the kid's gone runaway, good for him. If he's dead, then I don't care, as long as it's not in my driveway. Listen, I've got an old woman in intensive care, which could become a murder trial at any minute. I don't have the time or the patience."

He picked up his drink in a very dramatic way, like a moving exclamation mark, and drank it down in one go. It might have been impressive if it hadn't been half a pint of Coke.

"Besides," he said, "you get paid for this shit all the time. I just thought you could do with a push."

"A push?"

"Yes. Get you working for the right side again."

"Give me something, Beck. Why are you asking me to look into this?"

Becker sighed again. "I talked to his family, a few people at his university, classmates, lecturers. It just feels wrong.

Somebody is lying, and you were always better at smelling those than I was."

I asked for Perry's number. "Beck, tell me, what have you been hearing about drugs?"

He leaned back in the booth and eyed me for a minute. "So we get down to it. This about your brother?"

"Like I would give a shit about him."

"OK, what then? What have you got going on?"

"Just curious."

"Like you're ever 'just curious.' Look, I defend you all I can. I give you what information I can. But you work for the Mann brothers. I can't give you anything that gets back to those—" He paused. Becker had occasionally used racist terms when talking about the brothers, but he looked like he caught himself. He wasn't racist so much as white and middle class, but racism was a fluid thing in the Midlands. He settled for finishing the sentence with a milder insult, "Fucks."

"Give me more credit than that. I'm asking for me, just for me. I hear that the pieces are moving on the board."

"Well, that's more than I've heard."

"Seriously? You've heard nothing about a new seller? A Polish guy?"

He laughed. "Them Poles. They come over here, they steal our jobs, they steal our crime. Do they have no morals?"

"Just do me a favor and ask around for me, will you?"

He nodded.

If I took Becker's case, I could use it as cover, make it work for me. I'd have a reason to be walking around asking questions. It would protect me from attention while I looked for this Polish guy, and I could use it as an excuse to get information from Becker.

I left with a head full of missing students and dead women.

NINE

Next up, I decided to rattle another cage.

I'd already shaken the tree of the Mann brothers and had a gun pointed at me for my troubles. It was time to annoy someone on the other side and see what the response would be. I headed to Broad Street, the vice strip of the city. Fast food and smut. A dead body had recently been discovered in the kitchen of one of the street's restaurants, and nobody had been surprised. Above one of the kebab shops was a tattoo studio called Skin Art.

The reception area was a small room with a counter, like a hotel reception, and three doors opening off it. One of the doors was labeled "toilet," one wasn't labeled at all, and the other was ajar, the buzz of a tattoo gun coming from inside. The unmarked door opened and a lean teenage boy peered out, looked me up and down, and disappeared again. I stood there alone for a moment, listening to the tattoo underway inside and feeling awkward. The teenager appeared again, shutting the door behind him and taking up his best official-looking pose behind the counter.

"Sorry about your wait there."

"No problem."

"How can I help?"

It was my turn to look him up and down.

"Are you the artist?"

He laughed, taking my question as a joke. Of course he wasn't the artist—I doubt anyone would even trust him to write a name—but it had seemed polite to ask.

"I'd like to use your toilet," I said.

He looked me up and down again.

"Our toilet? Do you have an appointment?"

"I didn't realize I needed one. Last time I just turned up."

"You've been before?"

I was getting impatient with the whole game.

"Of course I have."

The buzzing in the studio stopped. A moment later a bald head peeped out from behind the door. Dave, the owner of the studio, was small and quiet. We'd met once before.

"Oh, it's you," he said. He nodded to the kid. "He's OK. Let him through."

He disappeared into the studio, and soon the buzzing resumed.

The kid moved out of my way, and I walked through the door that claimed to be the toilet. It opened onto a small corridor. The real toilet was little more than a closet that opened off this corridor. At the other end of the hall was an unmarked wooden door. It led to the building behind the tattoo studio, a private club known as Legs. It was a club owned by Ransford Gaines, the other big name in crime around here. Gambling, stripping, sex. You could get it all in here, and the prices were cheap because the club was off the books. There were no audits, no taxes, nothing declared.

You got frisked on the way in by two guys who looked like Russian wrestlers.

Once they gave you the OK and took your ten pounds, you were good to go. The first room you came to was a small casino, the top floor of an old building that had all but its supporting walls knocked through, making space for a bar that ran the length of the wall and tables for card games and roulette.

Down the stairs, on the ground floor of the building, was the strip club and the private rooms, the music rising up through the floor I was standing on.

This was the quiet time of day, as people were still at work out in the daylight. But many of the types who came in here didn't hold down your average nine-to-five job, so there was still a small crowd. I headed to the bar and ordered a straight whiskey. The size of a double for half the price. I celebrated with a second one.

"Hey, mate," I said to the barman. "Is Gaines in today?"

He gave me the fish eye.

"I don't know who you're on about."

I smiled and nodded and began to wander between the card tables.

"Hey," I said to a few of the people who made eye contact with me. "Seen Gaines around?"

I was being very subtle.

I walked down the steps into the strip club.

Down here it was very much a club, dark with flashing lights. Seedy and warm. As long as you didn't look too close at how cheap the drapes were or at the stains on the floor, you would buy the illusion. There is something silly about strip clubs. You can't take them seriously; you just have to switch off the rational part of your mind and go with it.

There's also a very male thing that goes on. Even if you go in full of moral outrage that women have to do this for a living, it all dies down the second you see a dancer walking toward you.

A cute but very made-up brunette walked up to me. "Hi, want some company?"

"Sure, your boss would do fine."

She shook her head as though I was a wasted opportunity, then walked away to find someone else. I continued to walk round. The club had an open floor plan: a small bar, leather sofas, and a small catwalk in the center. To the sides were curtained-off areas for private dances and doors for even more private things.

A few minutes and a few circles of the club and another woman stepped out in front of me. She was done up far more tastefully, subtle makeup and a dress that covered quite a lot of flesh. I figured she must be more senior than the other women, maybe not a dancer at all. I could smell the money in her perfume, as though it was the smell of molten gold.

"I'm Veronica."

"Hello."

"You've been making a lot of noise."

"I get that a lot, sorry."

"The boss will see you shortly. Why don't you let me get you a little more comfortable." She smiled a very nice smile, and somewhere deep inside I devolved into a schoolboy. "On the house."

I did my best Sean Connery smile, but I'm not Sean Connery, so I probably just looked nervous.

"Sure," I said.

She walked away ahead of me, doing that hip-swaying thing that I'm sure they practice. She led me into a private room and moved round behind me to shut the door. There was a glass of whiskey on a table, a larger measure than I had gotten upstairs, and a comfortable black chaise that was halfway between a bed and a sofa.

Veronica breathed in my ear and pushed me toward the sofa. I sat on the edge of it and helped myself to the whiskey.

"I don't suppose you're Polish, are you?" I asked.

She began to move to the rhythm of the music, very slow and slinky. She leaned in and kissed my forehead.

"I was just wondering, that's all," I said.

She was on her knees, and I had no idea how she'd got there without me noticing, dancing in front of me along the floor, crawling toward me.

"I mean, I'm not saying it's a deal breaker or anything."

I was surprised by how nervous I sounded.

Veronica's dancing was getting closer and more fluid. If you could make a cat into a human and name her Veronica, it would be much like this.

I'd given up the idea of being here on business, and I gave up any pretense of being a decent guy the second her mouth brushed past my crotch. As she rose up toward me, her hand brushed over my erection, and she flicked her eyebrow at me in just about the hottest way I had ever seen.

I was just thinking about being in her mouth and letting go when I was hit in the head from behind. The huge frame of a man stepped around in front of me as Veronica moved aside, smiling. He noticed my erection and punched it. Hard.

The spots dancing in front of my eyes prevented me from blacking out.

I hit the floor and rolled into a ball.

"Boss's ready to see you now," the man said.

TEN

The man dragging me along the hall was named Bull.

He was huge, which I assumed was where the nickname came from. He made your standard nightclub bouncer look like a midget. His size had led him to a number of jobs, from a seaside-resort wrestler in Blackpool to a doorman in London. These days he worked for Ransford Gaines, collecting money, delivering messages, and breaking legs. We knew each other professionally but didn't mix; Gaines and the Mann brothers had a long-established hatred of one another.

My breathing was returning to normal in small, rattled gasps. I'd managed to fight off the urge to be sick. I wanted to make it look like I was making an effort.

He shoved me shoulder-first through a door and down into a chair.

The office I was in was depressingly normal. It could have been the back office at any shop in the city.

"Hey, Bull." I nodded a greeting.

"Hey, Eoin." He nodded back.

"Did you really need to punch my cock?"

"Thought it would be funny," he said, without a trace of a smile.

"Hilarious," I said. The pain was still bad enough that I thought I might vomit.

A moment passed in silence before the door opened and Veronica stepped in.

She'd gone from stripper to office manager with one well-placed suit coat. She sat at the desk and smiled at me. Another moment passed before I realized what was going on.

"You're kidding me," I said.

"No, kidding you was what we did back there."

"You're in charge here?"

"Right now, yes."

"I need to speak to Gaines."

She leaned back in the chair and laughed. "I'd heard you were an idiot. I didn't realize how true that was."

The penny dropped. Everybody in the room probably heard it or saw the light go on above my head. I really am the slowest man in the world sometimes.

"Veronica Gaines?"

She nodded and did that flick of the eyebrow again. This time it didn't seem cute or sexy, this time I wanted to run for the hills. Veronica was Ransford Gaines's eldest daughter. She was regarded as the clever one. Her little sister, Claire, was the wild child. There had been rumors of the old man stepping back, spending more time at his big house in Solihull. Seemed it was more than rumors.

"So what was all that back there? The dance?"

"We thought it would be funny."

"That's just what Bull said."

"His is a dry wit."

We stared for a minute. I was resisting the urge to rub my crotch. I'd succeeded in rattling their cage, and it had got me a meeting with one of the Gaines family's senior members. I still wanted to play it cool, though. As cool as I could, considering I'd just been the butt of a very painful joke.

"I want to speak to your dad."

"Nobody gets to speak to him. You get me. Now what's this all about?"

"Drugs."

Veronica nodded to Bull, who gave me a rough patting down and checked under my clothes for a wire. I'd never known a cop actually to use one, but these guys watched TV, I guessed. I felt maybe I should start explaining to criminals in town that it would be the things they took for granted, like phones or computers, that police would tap.

After the search, I smiled my calmest smile and plowed ahead.

"I want to know about the new guy."

"The Polish guy? What do you know about him?"

"That he's Polish. And a guy."

"Then you know as much as we do."

"I find that hard to believe. He's taking your business. You'll have been looking for the dirt on him the minute he took a pound out of your pockets."

"Looking, yes. We've had a vig on his head for weeks. Got nowhere."

I wondered what reward they were offering. "You never asked me," I said.

"Eoin, if we could we would. But we both know we would never come to you, unless you fancy switching sides."

She knew I liked the eyebrow flick, she must have. That would be why she did it again. A firm offer to take dirty money from the Gaines family rather than the Mann brothers. I didn't really see a difference between the two that should concern me.

"I want to find this guy as much as you," I said. "If you're willing to pay me for that, I think I could smooth out my conscience."

"What's your stake in it? You've never taken an interest in drugs. Even the Mann brothers keep you out of it."

I avoided the question. It was still just as likely that Veronica or her dad had ordered Mary killed. I had to be careful.

"I hear your sister is using the product. Is it yours or his?"

Her face changed, the way daylight changes with the rolling in of a thunderstorm. "What that dumb chav does is not important to any of us."

Chav. It was one of the many words that the English language had stolen from Romani. To us, it just meant a young person, anyone under a certain age. In English, it was an insult, someone with no class or charm. Everything you need to know about the treatment of my people is right there.

Still, I'd hit a nerve. Good. I stored it away, filed under "fun."

"I only ask because it seems to be our new guy's approach to poach from you and the Mann brothers. I know he's been approaching your staff. Getting them working for both of you."

She nodded. "That matches what we've heard. You got any names?"

"Wouldn't give them to you if I had."

She digested this and seemed to make peace with it. The room was quiet again for a minute. Then she reached in a drawer behind the desk and threw a small wad of bills at me. I didn't count them, but they were twenties.

"You'll find this guy. You'll find who he is, where he is, and you'll lead us to him. After that, you'll walk away and leave us to it."

Like hell I will.

"Sure," I said. "I can do that."

If she didn't believe me, she kept it to herself. People that high on the food chain suffer from a strange form of vanity; they assume that if they throw money at people, then people will do what they're told.

And to be honest, I'd done little to disprove that theory.

The meeting was clearly over. I stood up to leave, only wincing slightly as I did.

"Eoin?" She gave me her nicest smile. "If you ever behave like that in our club again, we'll tear it off."

The pain dropped away as I shot a similar smile back. "Do I get another dance first?"

I left before she answered.

There was a much quicker way out of the club on the ground floor. But I felt the need to go out the way I'd come in. Smiling smugly at everybody I passed.

I was still in a lot of pain and had a nasty bruise spreading across a really unfortunate area. As a treat, using the money Veronica had given me, I bought an expensive bottle of whiskey and headed back to the flat.

After a long bath and some gentle rubbing, I sat with my brain in neutral through a few hours of very bad television. Then I cracked open the bottle but only took a few drinks to mellow myself out. I stared at the ceiling and aimed for a peaceful sleep. I was now working for both sides in the local drug war. How hard could it be?

ELEVEN

I called the Perry family from the flat that morning.

Becker had given me their home number, but they were both at work. The recording gave me the mother's work number and the father's mobile number.

The mother was my next call. Her name was Stephanie, and I found when I called that she worked at a school. She sounded more nervous than I'd expected. She asked if I'd be free to meet them in the early evening, to give them both a chance to get back from work.

She mentioned a few pubs. They lived in the area I had grown up in, so I knew them all. We settled on the Myvod in Wednesbury. It tended to have bouncers in the evenings and was away from the town center. It was the one least likely to have trouble or people I knew.

We agreed on five thirty.

I spent the morning looking for Jellyfish.

There was still no trace of him. A few people confirmed what Bobby had said, that Jelly was chasing tail and was probably holed up in whatever hideaway he'd managed to arrange. Well, he would have to come up for air at some point.

I had more luck finding Bauser. The Asian kid who'd led me to him before was standing around outside the bookie's. I told him I wanted to see his boss, and half an hour later he came and accidentally bumped into me as I was eating a cheeseburger on the street.

I followed him as before. This time Bauser walked up behind me, and we walked together through West Park, across the road from my house.

"Do you know where the new guy is?" I asked him after the usual handshaking.

He wasn't carrying a gun this time. Not that I could see, though his hoodie could have hidden a bazooka.

"Why the hell would I know?"

"Look, Baus. You know me. You know I've always been willing to keep your name out of things. I don't care what you have or haven't done. I don't care who you're taking your orders from. I just want to meet this new guy. I want to know his name and where I can find him."

Bauser was quiet as we walked along the lake. Lost in thought—or in ignorance.

"His name's Tommy. That's all I know. I don't know where he lives. He just shows up sometimes, and he calls me on my mobile."

"When was the last time?"

"Shit, I'm your secretary now? I don't know. Last week maybe. We haven't set anything up yet. He said he'd talk to me more next time he saw me."

"For you to switch gangs?"

"No. He wants people to work for both at the same time. Says it makes him money and makes his enemies lose money."

"So he doesn't want to get in a fight over territory?"

"Nah, man. He says taking territory is not as important as taking the people who stand on it."

Smart man, this Tommy. Somebody should introduce him to the gun-happy gangs over in Birmingham. There would be a lot less blood.

"Next time you talk to him, I want you to set up a meeting for me."

"How am I meant to do that?"

"Just tell the truth. Tell him Eoin Miller has been using his name all around town, and he's been asking for a meeting."

"Aren't you worried he'll kill you?"

"If he kills me, I'll have nothing to worry about."

I walked out of the park and crossed the road to my house and got into the car. I didn't need directions to my next destination. Fifteen minutes outside the city, it was the closest thing I'd had to a hometown when I was growing up. I listened to Bob Dylan's *Time Out of Mind* as I drove. The streets were deserted, and almost all of the shops were closed. Once the coal mines and factories had been taken away, suburbs like these had kept going through the life support of the service industry, but now that had gone too.

I drove past my old school, past places where I used to play football. It gave me a strange feeling that I hadn't expected. My childhood had been anything but normal, but then, we all fictionalize our childhood, get nostalgic for happiness we never had. I'd done a lot of my growing up in a pub. My mum wasn't Romani, and my dad drew a lot of heat for marrying a Gorjer. It wasn't an easy culture to marry into, and Mum wasn't accepted by many of the elders. She knew the problems her kids would face if they didn't play the game, so she talked my father into settling the family. Their solution was to buy a pub—one with a car park big enough for caravans if family wanted to visit—and we made a go at a normal life. They sent us to a local school, let us make friends and become part of the community.

It was always fake for my father, though, and he never settled into it. There were people in the town who never took to it either. The pub was set alight so often the firemen used to joke that we had them on speed dial. I still had nightmares sometimes about being woken up by thick black smoke and the sound of laughing kids.

The arsonists may have succeeded at some point, because as I drove past where my old home should have been, all I saw was a new housing estate. My memories felt as rootless as my blood.

I drove on through the familiar streets.

When I walked into the Myvod to meet the Perrys, it was nothing like I remembered. It had been full of brown wood paneling, with two separate bars, the way pubs used to be. The place I was in now seemed much bigger and brighter. The walls had been knocked through so that it was an open plan with the bar in the middle, and the remaining walls were painted in a neutral light beige. It looked like a large version of a very boring person's apartment.

The parents were easy to spot, they being the only couple sitting without alcohol in front of them. I sized them up as I bought a Coke at the bar.

Michael Perry looked a very different man than the overweight figure I'd seen on the job. He looked taller, probably because he was thinner. His face was still round, though, carrying traces of puppy fat that had never left. It lent him a youthful appearance. He was wearing glasses, thin-framed ones that were probably meant to make his face look narrower, and his clothes were expensive looking and smart. He looked like a casually dressed politician.

The mother had a faded beauty. I placed her as someone whose looks had probably peaked in school and gone downhill afterward. Her blonde hair was straight and worn to her shoulders around a face that didn't carry worry well. Her shoulders and waist showed more signs of age, with traces of extra weight that she wasn't comfortable with, her hands in her lap subconsciously covering her belly. She wasn't really overweight or unattractive; in better circumstances she would have been cute.

I tried to picture them as a couple twenty years ago, around the time they would have finished school or perhaps a year or two after that. She would have been very attractive for her age and probably considered above him, with his bookish, chubby looks.

He stood to greet me as I walked over to them.

"Mr. Miller," he said, waiting for a nod from me before he put out his hand. "I'm Michael Perry. This is Steph." I shook his hand and nodded to Stephanie.

"DS Becker spoke very highly of you, Mr. Miller," Stephanie joined in once we were seated. "He said you're the best person he's ever worked with at, well, this sort of—" She shrugged, avoiding the issue. "By the way, your first name is an unusual spelling, and you never said it on the phone. How is it pronounced?"

"Like Owen, but less E."

"Irish spelling?"

I nodded. "From my mum's family."

My mum's grandparents were Irish, and a few habits had stuck through the generations. My father named my brother and sister, but my mum named me.

Mr. Perry was apparently eager to get to the matter at hand, sitting impatiently through the small talk before trying to take control of the conversation. "I remember you on the force; you were good. Not very popular, though, with your family connections. Was that why you left?"

"No."

Most people had stopped trying to get me to open up about why I left, but Perry hadn't gotten the memo.

He finally took the hint and moved on. "And now you're private?"

For some reason I wanted to be blunt with this guy. "I work for the Mann brothers, Mr. Perry. But I'm sure you already know that." He didn't nod or say yes, but he didn't have to. "So what I'm wondering is, why not get the police involved officially? Surely you stand to lose out if people tie you to me. The press would love that."

"We like our privacy. I don't want to sound cryptic, but I have enemies on the force. I'm not sure opening myself up like that would be any help to Chris."

"Fair enough. I appreciate the honesty. I'll give you some advice now for free, and it could save you a lot of money."

They both looked at me in anticipation, wondering where my sales pitch was leading. I was wondering myself.

"Students run away. All the time. Usually they come back after a few weeks; sometimes they stay away for a few years. It's just the stress they're under or money that they owe or a girl that they're chasing across country. Hiring someone might make you feel better. But most likely? All it will do is drain your bank account."

I had amazed myself.

That was possibly the worst sales pitch in the history of anything.

They finished their drinks at the same time, and Michael looked at his wife.

"You want another?"

"No, I'll have something harder, I think—a vodka orange."

Michael looked at me and pointed to my glass, still mostly full.

"No, I'm all right, thanks," I said.

Michael had just stepped up to the bar when Stephanie looked after him and half stood up, saying, "I should remind him I don't want ice."

"Just waters it down," I said.

"No, well, I used to grind my teeth, and if there's ice in the glass…" She trailed off, shrugged, and sat back down.

In a minute, Michael came back with a bottled orange juice for him and a glass of vodka orange for his wife. She pulled a face at the ice in the drink but sipped it nonetheless. They seemed distant from each other, but I wasn't really in a position to judge other peoples' marriages.

"The thing is," Michael said, "we don't have a lot of money, but we need our boy found."

He put his hand on top of Stephanie's as if to emphasize the point, but it came off as a somewhat awkward gesture, not something they would normally do. She looked uncomfortable, like she wanted to snatch her hand away. This was a couple with problems, I could tell. Still. Their concern for their son felt real.

"How about this—I'll give you five days of the best I can do for three hundred pounds. If you don't like what I've found, or if you think someone else can do better, you can stop there and find someone else."

They looked at each other, having the wordless conference only parents can pull off. They turned to look at me at the same time, and Michael nodded.

"That sounds like a good offer."

This was without a doubt the strangest job interview I'd ever had. Perhaps I'd been doing it wrong all my life. Instead of trying to convince the interviewers that I was indispensable to their organizations and pension plans, I should have been telling them that the job they were hiring for was a waste of time and money.

"All right," I said. "Let's get started."

I pulled out my notebook and a pen.

Now I was working for two different crime families and a politician.

This kept getting better.

TWELVE

"So what do you need to know?"

"That's the trick," I said. "If we knew that, we'd know where your boy is. I need you to tell me who he was. I need to understand him to find him."

Stephanie nodded and looked briefly on the verge of tears. Michael hesitated before patting her shoulder, and I wondered if they ever normally showed affection in public.

"What was he studying at university?"

"Drama. From an early age he loved the idea of pretending, being different people. He always loved to dress up, to paint his face."

Michael cut in at this point. "But I've always been very keen to keep his head in the real world. I mean, acting isn't really a safe career path, is it? Particularly round here. Who wants to employ an actor with a Midlands accent? It's not like Wednesbury is Los Angeles."

"So you wanted him to do something else," I said.

"I wanted him to aim for something he could actually achieve," Michael said. "Business studies or law studies, even a bloody English degree would be more use, give him more options."

"Acting was what he wanted," Stephanie said. "He could have gone to another university, there are bigger ones with better drama departments, but to be honest I think he was nervous about moving too far away from home straightaway."

"So did he stay with you? Stay at home, I mean?"

"For almost a year, yes. He left somewhere toward the end of it. It wasn't a straightforward thing. He never announced that he was moving out, he just started spending more and more nights away from home, staying over with friends. And I never really noticed at the time, but soon he wasn't coming home at all, not for long stretches at a time."

"So how exactly did you know he'd moved out for good?"

"He came round one evening, at teatime, and rang the doorbell rather than letting himself in. Like he was visiting."

I turned my attention to Michael. "How did this sit with you, Mr. Perry? Had you noticed Chris wasn't coming home anymore?"

He paused for a beat, then started unsteadily, "Well, boys will be boys. I always tried not to pay too much notice to what he was doing."

"You didn't want to know what your son was doing?"

"What I meant is I know what boys are like. Especially when they hit that age, when they're old enough to drink and vote and do all the grown-up things. I know how they see the world. I always thought, leave him to it, leave most boys to it, and they'll sort themselves out in time. I'm just saying if Chris wanted to stay out all night, or for a week at a time, if he wanted to have a little fun, I wasn't going to get too involved in worrying about it."

I wondered if this had been a point of argument between husband and wife over the years.

"But you were quite keen to push him in other areas," I said.

"Of course I did. I didn't care if he wanted to have some fun outside of hours, but I wanted the best for him. I did my best to see him succeed."

"Would you say you put him under pressure at university? Did you push him to get results?"

"What are you getting at here? It seems to me you're implying I pushed him away."

"Not at all," I said, deciding to back off a little. "I just need to ask these questions to help build a picture of Chris in my mind."

I had hit a nerve with my last few questions, and I didn't want to set Michael against me so early.

"Mrs. Perry, would you say Chris was happy?"

"Happy?"

"Yes. It sounds like he had a lot happening."

She thought about it for a long time, watched closely by her husband.

"No," she said finally.

"No? So was he troubled? Was he sad?"

"I wouldn't go that far. Chris was never what you'd call happy, not really. He was always preoccupied with one thing or another. But he wasn't depressive or anything close to that, if that's what you mean."

"OK, tell me more. What did he enjoy?"

"Films." Stephanie smiled as she said it. "He loved films and television. If you started him talking about that sort of stuff, you couldn't shut him up again."

"Did he like football? Sports?"

"I used to take him to the games when he was younger," Michael said. "He was too young to remember the good times, and the bad times, in fact, but we used to go a lot."

"What else did Chris do? Did he like to party? You said you didn't want to stop him having fun."

"Oh, yes," Stephanie said. "He liked staying out, dancing, making a fool of himself."

"Drinking?"

"Of course. All boys round here like to drink."

I knew that was true enough. I'd been one of them for a long time. Drinking was a fact of life in this part if the world, just one of those things you did without thinking.

"Have you got the names or numbers of any of his friends from university?"

"Not off the top of my head, but I could get a couple," she said.

"That would be great. I'll need to talk to them. Did he have a girlfriend?"

"I don't think so, but he could have had one I never met."

"Do you know if he was on Facebook? Did he have a blog? Anywhere that he shared his feelings online could tell us more about where he might be."

"I don't think he had anything like that," said Mrs. Perry. "But then I don't know much about what kids do on the Internet."

I made a note to search for Chris online later.

Now I needed to hear from Michael Perry.

"You're high up in the force, and you're headed into politics," I said. "Anybody in particular who might want to cause embarrassment or hurt you?"

"I don't know."

Mark that avenue up as a big fat *maybe*. I needed to look into his career, see what was hiding in his closet.

"That should do for tonight," I said. "I've got enough to get started. Is it all right if I call round to your house in the next couple of days to get those phone numbers?"

They both nodded.

I asked if they had a photo I could use, and Stephanie gave me one that she had brought along. Chris was a good-looking kid, the best bits of his parents combined into a fair-haired teenager. As I looked at the photograph, Michael counted out the money I had asked for; they had come prepared. I wondered how much cash they had and wished that I'd asked for more.

I drove back to the city and let my mind turn back to my main problem.

Maybe I'd get lucky. Maybe I'd walk into my room and someone would hit me over the head, or point a gun at me at the very least, and announce that he had killed Mary and I was getting too close. I could be really lucky, and the person holding the gun would turn out to be our missing student.

Maybe, but I doubted it.

As I neared the outskirts of the city, the flashing lights of a police car loomed up in my rearview mirror and lingered. I tested my breath to make sure I wasn't going to get collared on a drunk, and a quick glance at the dashboard confirmed I wasn't speeding. I pulled over to the side of the road, and the car pulled up level with me. The uniform in the passenger seat rolled down his window, and I did the same.

"Mr. Miller?"

I nodded.

"You're hard to find. DS Becker says to tell you to check your phone messages once in a while. And asks you to follow us."

My own messenger service on wheels. Amazing.

The car pulled away, and I followed. The police led me to an isolated stretch of the canal, not far from the train station.

I parked and followed the uniforms. The blue lights were visible long before I reached the right spot, and they made my heart sink. I ducked under a police cordon, let through by a uniformed officer who recognized me, and looked for Becker.

"Thought you should see this," he said, calling me over to where a group of officers were huddled round something.

I didn't need to see much. I saw the poles and nets they'd used to fish a body out of the water. I saw a body bag.

Sticking out of it, darkened and heavy with water, was the sleeve of Bauser's hoodie.

Becker turned me away from the scene and the ears of others. "He was one of yours, right?"

"What time did you find him?"

"About forty minutes ago."

"How did he die?"

"Nothing official yet. But someone took a knife to him."

"He was just a kid."

"They all are."

My second body this week.

He'd still be alive if I hadn't gone looking for him.

How did it get to this?

I headed straight for Posada.

I put a drink to my lips.

Then it was a big black hole until waking up the next morning in the cold flat.

THIRTEEN

Next morning, as the sun made a halfhearted attempt at fighting with my curtains, I cooked what was left of the food in the fridge into a nice unhealthy breakfast.

I toyed with the idea of fetching the morning paper, but I didn't want to read about Bauser.

I didn't want to think about him, either.

The logic was too simple and painful. I suspected the Polish dealer of killing Mary. I'd asked Bauser to arrange a meeting, and Bauser was dead. My only solid lead died with him. I filed this away in the back of my head and tried to distract myself.

After breakfast I walked ten minutes into town, walking quickly because the cold air was biting, and headed to the police station. The reception desk was manned by the same PC as last time, and he seemed to brace himself as I walked through the door.

I gave him Becker's name, and mine, and said I was expected. He never took his eyes off me as he rang through to check, and even after he'd been told to let me through he made a point of checking my ID. Normally, a visitor would have to sign in, be given a pass, and be accompanied at all times. I got the feeling that Becker had given instructions not to make me sign the book, to keep my visit off the record, otherwise I'm sure the PC would have insisted on it.

Becker's desk was in an office shared with four other CID. I knew it well. It had been my office for a short time, and it could get very busy and loud in there. Right now, though, he was alone at his desk, waiting for me.

"You spoke to Perry, then?" This was as close as he was going to get to a greeting.

"I don't suppose you've got the official file lying around here, have you?"

Becker took his turn to smile.

"There is no official file, you know that."

"Good, so we won't be breaking any rules when you let me see the unofficial file, then."

Becker put a folder on the desk between us and then asked if I wanted a drink, saying he'd make a fresh pot of coffee. He was lying, of course; he'd be making me a cup of instant. Becker made the worst instant coffee in the world. But I nodded anyway. I needed to wake up, get my thoughts moving in a good direction. The file was unmarked and didn't contain any of the official forms you'd find in a police investigation. The notes too were written informally; none of the second guessing or neutral statements you'd find in a court-ready document. I read through them while he was away. There were interview transcripts, photographs, and details of the student's lecturers and friends at university. I jotted down names as I read.

Becker handed me a cup of coffee and I pulled a face at the first sip.

"So what do you think of it all?"

I shrugged. "The coffee? It's terrible."

He seemed annoyed, which I enjoyed.

"The kid," he said. "So you've spoken to the missing kid's parents? What about his friends?"

"Parents, yes. I don't know what to think yet, but there's just something about them—I can't put my finger on it."

Becker smiled. "You're into this now. I know that look in your eyes."

He fingered his pack of cigarettes idly, not even noticing he was doing it. The station had been made into a no-smoking zone when the laws changed, with a designated smokers' area out by the car park. People of all ranks huddled together. Smoking is a great leveler.

"I'm being lied to." He tapped the folder. "Someone in there was lying. I just don't know who it was or why. But it's there. Find out who and why, and you'll find the kid."

"But you can't spare the time."

"Exactly. Like I said in the café, I've got the acting DCI breathing down my neck to get the real cases cleared, and she doesn't know about this."

The previous DCI had retired recently and unexpectedly for health reasons. One of the most respected detective inspectors was filling in until the role was filled. The acting DCI was a woman, and that had ruffled a lot of feathers in the building.

"How's your case going with the pensioner?"

"She's still touch and go," Becker said. "The doctors don't know how she's going to respond yet."

"But you know who did it?"

"This guy—and I'm telling you I know he did it—he's got no more than three brain cells, he somehow managed to do it without leaving physical evidence. You tell me how it works? Kids with masks and gloves lifted a few TVs and toasters during the riots, and we were kicking their doors in three days later. One dumb fuck beats an old lady with his bare hands and I can't touch him. I mean, he's a moron, it has to be an accident, but he left no trace."

"Make this case and your career should get a bump up," I said. Becker had always been better at the ladder-climbing game than me. "What's happening with Bauser's case?"

His body faded a little in defeat.

"Nothing. Not a thing. Looks like a mugging, and he's known to have connections to drugs. Hell, look, he didn't make the front page of the newspaper. The old lady is a better human interest story for the press than the murder of a criminal."

"It could be gang related," I said. "The Mann brothers might push back and that would mean more blood. You're not investigating that?"

"Shite, mate. You think this is Birmingham? We're not treating this as a gang killing. Unless you can tell me otherwise?"

Yes.

"No."

"See? There's nothing there. If there's any payback from the brothers, then it will become a story. But when was the last time we had a gang war around here, huh? Our rates are good, and we're not going to do anything to mess with that."

There was no use arguing the point. After all, police who were willing to ignore the Mann brothers were good for my business.

I stood up.

"Cheers, Beck, and I do appreciate the work."

I was turning to leave when he smiled, and it wasn't a good smile.

"Wait, before you go. The acting DCI would like to see you."

Oh shit.

That meant talking to my wife.

FOURTEEN

It said a lot about Laura's skills that they'd given her a chance to fill in at DCI rather than transferring in cover from another office. She didn't have enough pull to get the job full time, but it was a good chance for her.

My name surely hadn't helped her find the way to the top. With my Romani background, I'd never been welcome in the force. Most in the ranks figured I only got in on positive discrimination, and they were probably right. Once I was in, I had to deal with racism and bigotry. More than once I opened my locker to find someone had taken a shit on my clothes or written messages on my paperwork. I'd like to say that behavior went away, but it never did. I simply learned to work with the good people and ignore the bad, which is how I met my wife.

As I sat down opposite her, I was reminded just how much better than me she had always looked. It's never mattered how much work I put into dressing up and grooming, there's always been something slightly scruffy about me, like the schoolboy who never looks comfortable in the uniform. Laura, on the other hand, always looked polished. Her hair was lighter than before, as if she was trying the slow crawl from brunette to blonde, and the few cute freckles on the bridge of her nose still called me out to play. First in uniform, now in business clothes, she always looked right, confident and poised, born for shiny hair and ironed clothes.

It was a nice office. The view wasn't much, but the office itself was well enough appointed. It had been repainted since I was last in there, with a new desk and Laura's personal touches added. She had plenty of photographs behind her—receiving diplomas, smiling in uniform—and a clipping from a newspaper. She didn't have any photographs of me anymore, which was both a relief and a pain.

"Eoin." The smile seemed genuine enough. "It's good to see you."

"Hi, Laura. You're looking good."

"And you, you've put on a bit of weight. It suits you. I always said you needed a bit more. Have you been keeping your appointments with Dr. Guthrie?"

"No."

"He wants to help, you know. That's what he's for. All you need to do is talk to him, talk about, well, you know."

Then the awkward silence. It was uncomfortable but expected. We'd split up in part to avoid these moments. I wondered for a moment who would be the first to crack and start some inane small talk.

"Have you been to see the Wolves play recently?" Laura cracked first, wanting to end the silence. I counted it as a moral victory on my part.

1–0.

"No, not at all this season."

"Oh. Bought any great albums you need to tell the world about?"

"No."

"How about Posada, are you still liking it there?"

"It's home, yes."

The awkward silence settled back over us. I didn't want to be here, I really didn't want to be here, and I didn't think she really wanted me here either. But there had to be a reason she'd asked.

"How are your parents doing?"

It was my turn to crack, point for Laura.

1–1.

"Fine," she said.

"They're probably busy showing off pictures of you and telling everyone how well you're doing. Nice office, by the way."

She blushed, and I tried not to smile.

2–1.

"Laura, why did you want to see me? It can't be because you miss me."

"No, I—" The silence halfway through a sentence is always familiar to failed couples. It gets to be like an old friend after a while.

"It's just…I know you're looking into the Perry case for Becker—"

"He thinks you don't know about that."

"I know, and I need to keep it that way. Listen, between us, this needs to go away quietly, and I can't let the department get involved."

"I still don't get why this is all so secret."

"Well, for Perry, this would be the end of him. Either his boy's dead, god forbid, or he's run away. Either of those would be too much damage to a political career."

"And for you? Why do you want it quiet?"

She paused and then shrugged a little bit.

"Perry is going to have a big say in who gets this chair permanently. A lot of the senior guys have been brown-nosing like you wouldn't believe. I can't be seen to get involved, one way or another."

"So this is all just about careers then, really."

"Don't be like that," she said. "I'm glad you're doing it. I think it's what you need."

"What I need? I'm not a charity case."

"Look, I'm not—I didn't mean it that way. It's just that this seems safer than—"

"What," I said wearily.

"Than what we both know you've been doing since you left."

"Look, I don't know what you've been told or who you've been talking to, but—"

"Eoin, I didn't ask you in here to argue about this. I know who you've been working for, and I'm glad you're giving something else a try. I think it's a good thing you're getting some distance from the brothers."

There was a look that passed between us as she said that, something I almost didn't catch in the movement of her eyes. It hung between us for a moment.

"Are you warning me off the Mann brothers?"

"I'm not warning you off anything."

"Laura, are you planning something? Is the department going to move in on their operation?"

"Don't be silly. There's no way we could get permission on something like that."

"Well, a big collar like that, it might get you this job permanently. It would make a good case anyway."

"Don't be silly. We both know I'm too young and too female to get the promotion this time around."

I nodded. "But filling in like this will be earning you the points you need for next time, when you're older and less female." I counted that as a score to me.

3–1.

"And really, what you're asking me to do with Perry is do the right thing by you. You want credit if it goes well, and you want it buried if it goes bad, right?"

There it was again, and this time there was no missing it, the look passing between us. A warning. I realized it was best to take it and not to push.

"Well, it's been fun," she said, reaching for her phone. "I've got appointments. See you soon, Eoin."

Just like that she was dismissing me from her office, and I was getting up to leave. How is it that we let women have that power? Maybe it's a mother thing, I don't know, or maybe they have some hidden abilities. All I know is that most women can make any man feel like a naughty child with one turn of phrase.

That's worth a hat trick, right there.

4–3 to Laura Miller.

FIFTEEN

I felt sheepish.

I decided the best way to get back at her was to visit our marital home and kick the crap out of something she'd liked. That wasn't my first order of business, though. The main point of the trip was to go to pick up my savings. I wasn't raised to trust banks. I was taught to have a roll of cash nearby and a packed suitcase just in case. Even during my marriage, I'd had a bag packed and hidden away.

As I pulled my car onto the drive and looked at my house, my breath caught in my throat.

The door was open.

And Bobby was sitting on the step, waving at me.

"They broke in, Eoin."

"Who? Who broke in?"

"I don't know who it was. They were gone when I got here."

"When was this?"

"Last night, when I came looking for you."

"Wait, hang on, go over it for me."

I was in the house now, checking the hallway. I don't know what I was expecting to see.

"I was looking for you last night—"

"What time was this?"

"No, it wasn't that late, would have been about nine, maybe half past. So I was walking past, and I saw the door open, just a little, not wide open like it is now."

The kitchen had been trashed; the fittings had been torn off the wall, and the floor was littered with smashed plates. The fridge was unplugged and pulled away from the wall. The sink was full of food and milk, the contents of the fridge all removed from their wrappings and tipped out. My collection of herbs and spices was scattered across the floor, the jars stomped on and smashed. The back door, which opened off the kitchen, was also wide open.

Someone had done a very thorough job of looking for something. The advantage they had over me was that they knew what they were looking for. Nobody knew about my savings, not even Laura, so it had to be about Mary.

"So what did you do?" I was in shock over the mess. At least I had Bobby to tell me a few details.

"Well, I was scared, to be honest," Bobby said. "I didn't know who'd done it or if they were still here. So I stood in the doorway for probably ten minutes."

"That happens a lot in this situation," I said. Over the years in the force I'd noticed that people who weren't used to seeing real crime always seemed shocked when they came face-to-face with it.

"So then I came in and started looking round," he said. "I saw what they'd done to the kitchen and went upstairs to take a look."

"So whoever it was had left by then, by half nine?"

"No. I thought they had, but they must have still been in the house. See, remember I said I looked in the kitchen first?"

I nodded.

"Well, the back door was closed. When I came back down from upstairs, the back door was open. So they had still been in the house when I first came in. I bet they stood and watched me standing in the doorway for ten minutes, staring off into space like a moron."

I didn't have any problem picturing that image.

"So they must have done upstairs first, then been doing the kitchen or the living room when you showed up?"

I checked the living room; it was a mess, but not as much as the kitchen. Shelves had been pulled away from the wall; the carpet had clearly been pulled up because it lay loose under my feet. I left Bobby on the sofa while I checked upstairs. The bathroom was a disaster site. The bath was cracked; there was water all round the toilet. In the bedroom, the bed had been turned over, the mattress slashed. A section of wall, where the wallpaper had been bubbled and loose, had been punched through to reveal the bad plastering job covering an old fireplace.

What the hell had they been looking for?

One thing I hoped they hadn't found was my savings. If you're ever going to hide money, never put it under a loose floorboard. Loose floorboards are loose. They make noise, they move, anyone seriously doing over a house will find them. I found the flat-headed screwdriver I kept in my bedside drawer. I knelt to the skirting board, stuck so firmly to the wall that it was about the only thing in the room the searchers hadn't moved. I worked the head of the screwdriver into the gap between the board and the wall, a gap that was only there if you knew what you were looking for. It took me a few minutes to pry the board loose. The wood glue and nails I'd used to stick it back to the wall in the first place wanted to fight. I put the screwdriver in my coat pocket and pulled the wood loose. As I pulled the roll of money out of the cavity, I heard a cough at my shoulder—Bobby standing over me.

"What you got, Eoin?"

How long he'd been there I had no idea. I'd played football with him a couple of times, and though you had to shout constant instructions at him, he moved like greased lightning. He'd make a great ninja.

"Just my cash, Bobby. How long you been there?"

"Oh, not long. I heard noises and thought, I don't know, it goes through my mind maybe the people were still here or something. Maybe you needed help."

"So what did you do next? After you found out they'd just left the house when you got here?"

"Well, I waited for you. You're not easy to get hold of at the moment. You haven't got a mobile. Even my granny has got a mobile, but not you."

When I'd quit my job I'd found that I didn't want to be reachable. It had been easy enough to lose my mobile, and then I kept finding excuses not to replace it.

"So you just waited for me?"

"Yes."

"You waited here all night and all morning for me?"

"Yes."

"But, Bobby, you knew where I was. You gave me the keys to one of the spare flats, remember?"

It took a moment, but a slow grin spread across his face.

"Oh yeah." He shook his head. "I did."

I slipped a couple of notes off my roll and handed them to him. He'd earned it. I pulled off a few more notes and handed them to him too.

"You could do a few things for me, if you're available?"

He took the money and nodded.

"OK, first things first, I'm going to need this place cleaned up. You could get some supplies from town and get this place fixed up."

"Sure, sounds good."

"Great. Thanks, Bobby. The other thing I need is a mobile. Get me a decent one. No contract, though."

Bobby nodded and took the hint, turning to leave.

"One other thing," I shouted after him. "Why were you looking for me?"

He turned back and stared at me for a moment. As usual, it took a little while for the information to run around the inside of his brain.

"Jellyfish. I haven't been able to find him. Some guys reckon he's over in Walsall, maybe."

Bobby waved and left. I heard him walk down the stairs and shut the front door after himself, then the sound of mail hitting the floor.

I walked downstairs to find the mail from the past few days in a pile on the floor. It must have been pushed up against the wall, hidden by the open door. It looked like the usual collection of reminders, bills, and junk. There were two more from Dr. Guthrie. I added them to the pile marked with his return address that I kept ignoring. Most of the mail was the usual bland white envelopes. One envelope caught my eye, though, a brown A5. It didn't have a postmark or an address written on it.

It had been hand delivered.

I opened it and tipped the contents out onto the floor.

Photographs. Black-and-white, high-quality photographs. The first two showed Mary and me as we walked home, then the moment she opened the front door with my key. The third showed Mary's body in the state I had found it, wrapped in my bedsheets. There was a fourth, and that was the one that made my blood run cold.

It was a close up; it showed me leaning over the body.

From the angle, it looked like it had been taken by someone standing in the doorway to my spare room. Someone who had still been in the house when I found the body.

The message was clear. The killer could fuck me over anytime he chose. And he'd torn my house apart looking for something. I should probably have reacted in fear. After all, I'd panicked and run away like a git once already this week. Instead I did something that even I didn't expect.

I laughed.

Out loud.

I'd been wasting my time looking for the killer. I'd been making a lot of noise and leaving a trail. But the whole time, the killer was looking for me, or at least for my stuff. He thought I had what he wanted. Because whatever Mary had stolen from him was still missing. He didn't have it, and it seemed like he thought I did.

I didn't need to find the Polish dealer.

I needed to find whatever he was looking for.

And I needed to find it before he framed me for murder.

SIXTEEN

With Bauser gone, I needed Jellyfish more than ever.

Bobby had said Jelly was in Walsall.

Like most towns in the area, it was within a twenty-minute drive. But the way Bobby had said it you'd think Jelly had fled to Mexico. We can be a very parochial bunch round here. Our borders are important to us.

Driving back into the town was like slipping into an old shoe; it was another of the towns I'd spent a lot of my youth in, being one of the main drinking spots and where I'd been based when I was in uniform. Walsall's a town, and it moves at town speed. Slower than Wolverhampton, it has fewer face-lifts and a thicker accent. The town center was crumbling. Where once there had been major chain stores, I saw more and more discount shops and building projects standing half-finished. Large parts of the Midlands had never recovered from the collapse of industry, and Walsall was a clear sign of that, except for a few chosen streets where the money was spent in fashionable bars.

This had made drunkenness into the town's biggest business. The pubs were constantly being bought out and repainted. The names were changed, the themes updated. But no matter how many times a pub was themed or cleaned up, the drinkers stayed the same.

I wandered from pub to pub, making greetings with forgotten names, making conversation with people I knew. Any questions about Jelly were coming up empty. I settled in at the Wheatsheaf, which had once been my regular pub. It used to be a very worn, lived-in rockers' pub. It had a nicely predictable jukebox and the occasional good ale. Now there were white walls, framed pictures, and leather sofas arranged around a lot of confused rockers. I struck up conversation with the new owner, a large man with big ideas. We were talking about what he'd done to the place and what state the wiring had been in, when Jellyfish walked in.

I didn't see him at first—I'd been too involved in the conversation to be watching the door—but I felt a hand on my shoulder and Jelly's voice.

"Why you looking for me, Eoin?"

I smiled. Finally.

"Can't I just look up an old friend?"

"Friend? Is that what you're calling it? Man, you only come to me when you got questions or when you want to bust me about something."

"Don't take offense, Jelly, I'm like that with all my friends. Hell, you should see the way I treat my family."

He laughed. "From what I've heard, your family don't ever talk to you."

I must have flinched. I saw it in his eyes. "Well, you know how it is. It's not any fun unless you're the black sheep."

I ordered him a pint of lager, and we moved over to sit on one of the sofas.

"Who told you I was looking for you?"

"My man."

"His name being?"

"You wouldn't know him."

"And I never will unless you tell me who he is."

"Friend of mine. Maurice. He spoke to you. Well, I think more like you spoke to him. Talked to him like you used to get on back in the day, whichever day that is, since he's my age and you're older than both of us, but he knew who you were."

I was pretty sure I didn't know any Maurice.

"Describe him to me. I don't know the name."

"You're not going to go looking for him?"

"No, don't worry. I just don't like people knowing who I am if I don't know who they are. It makes me nervous."

"Tall, tallish anyway, he's got short hair that stops about a shade short of being ginger, and the man is fat."

"How fat?"

"Well, you don't normally like to say when it's a friend of yours, but this kid is fat, and I'm not talking puppy fat. Can't be puppy fat, he's twenty-seven. Guy looks like he's in training for the belly Olympics, and he's going to take gold."

"But you don't like to say about friends."

"Well, OK, he's more what I'd call a passing acquaintance."

"Uh huh."

"Yeah, just a guy I know."

I knew who he meant.

This Maurice had been propping up the bar in the Walsall Arms. He'd been nursing a Guinness as if nursing was about to become illegal, and I'd believed him when he told me he'd never heard of a guy called Jelly.

And he wasn't just fat; he was terminal.

"You know why I'm here, Jelly."

"No, I don't. I don't know anything at all, man, and you can quote me on that. You can quote me on that and write it in big black letters, in a very good paint, across the north bank at Molineux. I don't know anything."

"OK, Jelly, don't worry. I won't be telling anyone where I got it from. Is this why you're holed up in Walsall?"

"What? No, no, man. I'm just taking it easy, got friends round here."

"One friend in particular from what I hear."

He grinned and did a fake modest shrug.

"Well, yeah, you know."

"Fill me in, will you. What the hell has been going on?"

"Well, I really don't know it all. I mean, I know bits and pieces, but bits and pieces don't make a lot of anything."

"Just start talking," I said.

Jelly would always talk, no problem. The trade-off would always come later on, or he'd hold it over you like a credit note.

"Well, it starts with the Poles, you see. All them fucking Poles. You notice how everybody in town's got Polish accents these days? Don't know what the hell's going on."

"Poland joined the EU."

"Well, yeah, I do know. I'm just saying."

"OK."

"Well, see, it's been tense for years, you know that. You got the Mann brothers handling the Asians, working some real miracle shite, keeping the Indians and the Pakis on the same page." He paused, looked at me, then corrected the slur. "Pakistanis, I mean. Anyway, they're all young, they see the business side. Then you got Gaines sitting on top of the older money, the Irish connections, all that. They've been managing to ignore each other and stick to their own shit. They're happy enough to split the pie as long as the Birmingham gangs stay out of it. Anyway, this Polish guy, Tommy, he turned up fresh off the boat."

"Most likely the Eurostar."

"Yeah, man, I'm just *saying.*"

"OK."

"And he starts talking around town about meth and heroin, like some all-you-can-eat buffet. Before you know it, he's selling crystal to Claire Gaines, and her old man is shitting a brick about it."

Claire Gaines. Veronica's little sister.

"But it isn't just that. He's getting his hands on loads of this shit. He's selling junk, he's selling methadone, for fuck's sake, on the street, and he's got his own supply lines. That's where the money is, man, prescription junk. Meth and heroin are just the salad dressing, and he's practically giving those away. Using them as calling cards, yeah? The junkies love him, man. He's like Robin Hood or Jesus or something."

"I don't think either of them was a drug dealer."

What Jelly was saying made sense. Prescription drugs were gold dust. Biggest slice of the trade in Europe and not cracked down on in the same way as good old-fashioned rock-star drugs. You didn't need grow-ops, chemists, and guns—you just needed a few contacts in the import trade and a knowledge of how to fiddle paperwork. A man could get rich fast.

"It's just basic business, man. He's selling good product at a cheaper price. I mean, I got offered some, I saw the goods, it was legit, and he was practically giving it away."

"Saw it? You mean you met him?"

"Yeah, man, he bought me a drink in the Apna, wanted me to get him more pushers. That's the other thing he's doing. He's getting the existing pushers in his pocket."

"OK, describe him to me."

"Nah, wouldn't help."

"Why not?"

"I'm getting to it."

"OK."

"So what you got, see, is this new guy turning up and getting people onside. The coke and heroin reel people in, then he starts to talk about the serious money he can spin with the prescription shit. But he hasn't made nice with the brothers or Gaines. Hasn't bothered to work points with any of them. He just turns up and starts selling this shit at lower prices, on the same corners, through the same people."

"OK."

"So Gaines is pissed as hell."

"You mean Veronica. Yeah, I know her."

"She's hot. Anyway, she's offering money to people to kill this Tommy, and you've got both Gaines and the Mann brothers wanting to take their business back."

"They all want his supply route."

"Exactly. I mean, I'm sure that was a far bigger thing for Gaines than protecting his youngest daughter's nose. I mean, family is one thing, but this is money."

"So Gaines and the Manns are both asking around town about this guy?"

"Yeah."

I wondered why the brothers hadn't brought me in on this. It was the sort of thing I'd have been perfect for.

"Then, about two weeks ago, he gets busted."

"Arrested?"

"Yeah, little Tommy Tucker, the silver spoon, you know the book? That was set in Poland, wasn't it? The kids with the silver spoon in a box?"

"Sword. *The Silver Sword*."

"Yeah, I know, I'm just saying. He gets caught red-handed in the Apna, selling drugs. Busted for possession like a common dealer."

This was news. If Tommy had been arrested, there would be a file. There would be a record and criminal charges. Becker could tell me all I needed to know.

"But he must have gotten out, right?"

"Well, we never heard about no court case or bail, so it doesn't sound like he was held on a charge, but he just vanished after that."

"Vanished? Vanished in what way?"

"Well, we don't know. Just in that he's not around. And a lot of people are asking about him on the streets."

"What people?"

"Well, you."

"Yeah."

"The pushers, all the people he'd set deals with. They're asking. Bull was asking for the Gaines family, and that Robson guy, he was asking around a lot too."

"Robson?"

"Yeah, you know, Mr. Robson, the other guy who works for the brothers."

"Never heard of him."

"Ah, c'mon, I've seen you with him."

OK, I'd work on that one later. I didn't want to lose the thread.

"What were they asking?"

"People want to know where he's staying and where his stash house is at. Eoin?"

His voice was different now. Softer. There were no jokes in his voice, just hurt. He continued when I looked at him.

"Killed Bauser, man."

Now I realized this talk might not come with a credit note. Bauser and Jelly had come up together in the scene, Bauser in the gangs and Jelly at the parties. Always mixing, never quite friends. But I could tell Jelly cared, at least a little bit.

"I know. I saw his body."

"You know who did it?"

"Not yet."

I dropped a twenty-pound note on the sofa between us and excused myself to go to the toilet. I had to laugh when I got in there. The owner had clearly spent a lot of money renovating the pub, but the toilet was still exactly the same as it always had been, graffiti and all. When I got back to the sofa, Jelly had left and taken the money with him.

I downed my Coke and followed.

Out on the street, I couldn't see Jelly. I'd taken a big gamble by giving him such a head start. I really didn't think he had any more to give, but I wanted to know where he was staying. Then I heard his voice, to my left, a little farther up the hill and just out of sight. I walked to the bend and saw him walking away up the hill, talking to a woman as he went. From behind, all I could make out was that she was the same height as he and blonde. They paused to cross the road. I thought they were going to spot me when they looked back for coming traffic, but somehow they didn't. I crossed in the same direction after they were out of sight and hurried to turn into the road they'd walked up.

We were by the church now, right at the top of the town. I watched them walk across a car park and up to an old set of low-rise flats. I stood in the shadow of a tree and watched which flat they went into, then turned and retraced my steps back to my car.

SEVENTEEN

I drove back to the flat. It felt more natural than the house now.

Bobby had left a package there for me, on the coffee table. There was a bundle of receipts for paint and tools. I guess he was used to having to prove his expenses to the Mann brothers. There was also a mobile and a note telling me he'd topped it up with fifty pounds' worth of talk time.

I was back in circulation.

I keyed in a number I just about remembered and listened to it ringing for an age before it was answered.

"Hello?"

"Beck? It's Eoin."

"It's my day off."

"Yeah, so listen, you got a minute?"

"Eoin, it's my day off."

"I've run into a few things. There's this case I've been looking into and—"

"It's the day that comes at the end of the working week? It's very precious to those of us with proper jobs."

"I could really do with some background."

"Is this anything to do with the misper you tried reporting at the station the other day?"

I weighed the options. I could lie and have him know I was lying. I could tell the truth and he still might not help me. Weigh the options, weigh the odds.

"Yes."

"And will you tell me what it's all about?"

I didn't need to lie. Because I didn't yet know the truth.

"I'll tell you as much as I can. Can you trust me on that much?"

"All right, what is it you need?"

"Drugs. Drugs in town. I've been told a few stories about a Polish national moving into Wolverhampton at cheap prices. I've been hearing about Gaines and the Mann brothers taking an interest. The guy's name is Thomas, or something like it, maybe a Polish variation on it."

There was a pause on the line. Too much of a pause. I'd touched on something familiar. Finally he spoke.

"Jesus."

"Any of this sound familiar?"

"I'm going to have to look a few things up."

"OK. And, Beck, why is this the first I've heard of it? Why hasn't the press got a taste of this and made it front-page news?"

"I'll add that to my list of things to look into. Eoin?"

"Yes?"

"This sounds, uh, big."

"Tell me about it."

"And this might take a while. I'll call you when I've got something."

"Any idea when that'll be?"

"Probably not on my day off."

Fair enough. There was silence on the line for a moment.

"Eoin? How are you getting on with the missing student?"

I paused too long before answering. "Fine," I said, too late.

"You've not done anything, have you?"

"Well, this other thing I've got, it's kind of important, you know? I'll get round to it."

"Jesus, Eoin, you've taken their fucking money. I need you to come through on this, to do the right thing. Have you forgotten what that's like?"

"That's a bit harsh."

"No. No, it isn't. Listen, you've taken on the job, you're going to *do* the job. You want the information from me, you'll have to get the work in on the student."

He hung up.

Bollocks. I hated it when he was right.

I phoned the University of Wolverhampton, and the receptionist put me through to Chris Perry's tutor. He said he could see me right away, and I drove into town to get there quicker. He was waiting for me at the reception desk. He shook my hand and introduced himself as I filled out the visitor's pass and was allowed through.

His name was Paul Lucas. He was a skinny, middle-aged man with short red hair and absolutely no smile whatsoever. He led me through the building and out into the central courtyard, where he stopped to ask some students why they hadn't handed their assignments in. Then we continued on to his office on the third floor of the Millennium Building. The building had been erected around the turn of the century to house displaced members of staff from closed campuses in nearby towns. A lot of brick and glass, it had no library but two coffee shops.

Lucas's office was a cramped space that he seemed to share with two other lecturers. The room was dull and gray, and the window showed a view of the ring road, the circular dual carriageway that encircled the city like a concrete moat. I decided that a career spent in this room would drive a man to murder, and I hoped I wasn't right. We both sat down, and Lucas tried his best smile.

"So you're working with the police?"

"No."

"Oh. I thought—"

"Sorry if I gave you that impression. I'm working private—I've been hired by Christopher's parents to find him—but both DS Becker and DCI Miller will vouch for me, if you need it."

"No, it's fine. Whatever helps."

I pulled my battered old notebook out of my pocket and flipped it open. It's a useful tool if you want to unsettle someone.

"When was the last time you saw Christopher?"

"I last saw him, let's see—I wrote all this down when the police were asking." He pulled out a pad that had notes written on it in very small, very neat handwriting. "I last saw him three days before he disappeared."

"What mood was he in when you saw him?"

"Positive. Chris was always very positive."

"Did he have anything here at university that might make him run away?" I leaned forward. "I mean, did he tell you anything that might help us?"

"No, nothing I can recall. Certainly nothing that would be worth giving it all up."

"He wasn't behind on work?"

"No. He used to be. When he first started here he had a lot of trouble with deadlines, with attendance. We thought he might not make it through his first year. But this year he's really come into his own, hands everything in on time, gets decent grades."

"Is that common?"

"Oh, sure. To be honest, we get all kinds here. Some students start well, then fall apart. Some start badly, then grow up. Chris was one of those, I think."

"Was he a good actor?"

"He was OK. He's never going to be a big star, and I think he knows that. But, and this has really started to come out in this last semester, he's quite a talented scriptwriter. I think with another six months, he'd have realized that was what he should be pursuing."

"Writing?"

"Absolutely. He was very polished. He was a natural at pacing, at leaving the right amount of room for the actors."

"What sort of things did he write?"

"Comedies, really. Subtle comedy, more grown-up than his classmates."

"So he wrote feel-good stuff? Happy endings?"

"I'd say he wrote simple rather than happy. He liked straightforward plots, a conflict and a resolution, simple characters. Writing simple is something we spend most of our time here trying to get through to them. He has that naturally."

"Chris was in a lot of your classes?"

"Yes, he's been in a few of mine. I don't teach the practical side of acting. I deal more with the other side. I go through how to approach scripts, how to break them down and research them, how to block the scenes. Like I said, it was that side of things that Chris was really starting to grow."

"In your classes?"

"Well, yes."

"How about personal problems? Did he have a girlfriend, any problems there?"

He paused. Not much, but enough for me to notice.

"No. He didn't have a girlfriend. He didn't seem to let things like that get to him. Not like some of the kids we get here who seem to come just to pull, like it's one long game of kiss chase."

"How about his parents? Did Chris feel pressured or harassed? Were there any arguments there?"

"I thought it was his parents who hired you. Should you be asking about them?"

"I've got to ask about everything. Do you think they were an issue?"

"No, I—look, all students feels pressured by their parents. Whether their parents are actually doing anything or not, they feel it. I wouldn't say that's worth looking into here."

I wrote his responses down in my own scruffy version of shorthand. I wanted to see if I could force an error from him. Writing notes in front of him was a simple way to do that.

"Did he have any enemies on campus, anyone who might feel the need to hurt him or who might make him leave?"

"None."

"And he didn't drink too much?"

"Oh no, he didn't drink at all. Chris didn't touch alcohol."

Strange. That didn't fit with what his parents had said. I noted it in the book and circled it. I noticed the tutor's gaze follow my pen as I did. "So what's your take on it? What do you think has happened to Chris?"

He looked out of the window for a moment before answering, watching the traffic crawl around the ring road.

"Honestly, I think he's OK, and I think he'll come back when he's ready, if we leave him to it."

"Why? You said he had no problems."

He hesitated again, holding something back.

"Well, nothing big, no, but all kids need time sometimes. You know, a break."

"Isn't that what their semester breaks are for?"

"Well—"

"Mr. Lucas, is there anything else you should be telling me?"

He looked straight into my eyes as he shook his head, leaving a pause between that and answering. I wondered if he used to smoke, the way he kept leaving gaps between thoughts like smokers will when they've got a cigarette in their hands. Some people can give up smoking but never give up the habits that go with it.

"Nothing," he said.

I stood up to leave, pocketing my notebook. "OK," I said. "Thanks for your time. I'll be in touch with more questions."

"Please book in advance." He shook my hand again. "My days fill up pretty fast."

"One last thing. Did you used to smoke?"

"Why, yes, I did." He paused. "I stopped about two years ago. Why?"

"No, no reason." I smiled it away and left.

He knew something. It was obvious, hanging in the air.

If you want to tell what someone's reaction is when they lie, get them to tell the truth. The pause as he recalled how long ago he'd quit smoking, the length of time it took him to access the truth, told me that he'd been lying to me with his other answers.

EIGHTEEN

The afternoon had drifted into early evening by the time I got back in the car to drive to Wednesbury. I flinched at the bad smell as I got in and turned the key. The floor was littered with old meal wrappers and empty drinks cartons. I couldn't remember the last time I'd picked it up or washed it, but I must have left some fried chicken in the back or something. Something else to add to my list.

I took a longer route than needed because I wanted a little breathing space. I drifted around the main roads and backstreets for a while, guided by the goddess of traffic lights and guitar chords.

Music helps me think.

I listened to an old mix CD, Lou Reed taking turns with Marah and the Twilight Singers. It all seemed perfect as I coasted around the town I'd grown up in, the town I couldn't seem to escape from anymore. The town took its name from the pagan god Woden, a heritage that predates anything the Christians had to say. "God's Town," my father would always call it as a joke. There had been a fort dedicated to Woden, sitting on top of the hill that dominated the town, but now that space was taken by two churches, sitting in judgment on everything below.

Johnny Cash singing "I See a Darkness" with Will Old-
ham. Acoustic confessional, scary and honest. Johnny Thunder's "You Can't Put Your Arms Around a Memory." Even
stripped down and acoustic, it was still a sing-along, but my
voice threatened to drown out Thunder's. I crossed over old
abandoned train tracks and past empty husks that were factories when I was younger. I drifted into "Crown of Thorns" by
Mother Love Bone. I didn't even remember owning that one,
long and miserable, with piano that builds followed by loud
and glorious guitar that rips the song a new one.

I pulled into the street where the Perry family lived and
parked at the top. I could see the living room light was on
as I approached, and a car was on the drive. I rang the doorbell and waited for a full couple of minutes before the door
opened an inch, on a chain, and Stephanie Perry peered out
at me. Her expression was blank for a second until she recognized me.

"Oh," she said. The door shut, and I heard the chain
move. Then the door opened wide, and Stephanie smiled
at me.

"You didn't call," she said as she stepped aside so I could
enter. "Sorry, I wasn't expecting you."

"No, I'm sorry. Is it a bad time?"

"Oh no, no. Not for you. Is it good news?" I could see the
hope framing her eyes.

"Not yet, I'm afraid. That's why I'm here, for more
information."

I followed her into the living room, a brightly decorated
space with photos of Stephanie and Chris, one of him in a
Wolves football kit. My parents had similar photographs of
me as a child. She waved me onto the sofa and asked if I'd
like a drink. I asked for a strong coffee.

While she was gone, I examined the room at closer
detail. It was a very feminine room. The furniture and the

decorations, the way the photographs were positioned—
they all showed a woman's touch. The only thing that really
seemed like it might have been added by Michael or Chris
was the widescreen television taking up a whole corner of
the room.

Stephanie walked back into the room carrying two
steaming cups.

"Sorry, Michael's not back from work. We could have
arranged for him to be here if you'd called."

I apologized again and sat down with my drink.

"So you've got more questions."

"A few, yes. First I'd like to go back over one or two
things."

She nodded. I sipped my coffee, pleasantly surprised
that it was good.

"You said that Chris liked going out, liked having a good
time?"

"Yes. Not so much lately, I think, but he's always liked
going out."

"And part of that is drinking?"

"Yes, like we said, all boys round here like a drink or
two."

"But not to excess?"

"Not enough to be a big problem, if that's what you're
asking." I noted the defensiveness in her voice and an empty
tumbler glass on the table next to her chair.

"It's just that someone else told me today that Chris
didn't touch alcohol."

"Well, I can tell you Chris drank. I can also tell you it
wasn't a problem."

I gave her my nicest smile, trying to let her know I didn't
doubt her.

"How about Mr. Perry? Michael? I noticed at the pub he
was drinking orange juice. Does he stay off the booze?"

"Michael stopped drinking a few years ago. It got in the way of his ambitions. You know how it is."

"Where would you two go out, back when he was drinking? Local? The city?"

She paused and then turned the tables on me. "Why?"

"No reason. My parents used to run a pub just down the road, the Wagons Rest. Did you know it?"

"Oh, yes, we went in there quite a lot." Then her eyes widened a little as she put two and two together. "Oh, you're one of the boys, Erica's children, right?"

"That's me. Us."

"You were such wild kids, I remember. How's your brother doing? And your sister?"

"Honestly, I have no idea." I didn't like talking about my family, so I changed back to the subject at hand. "How are you holding up?"

She relaxed at this, leaning back into the chair and finally letting the mask drop away. I felt as if it was really the first time I'd met her, and she looked tired.

"It's hard," she said. "It's so hard. My baby's out there somewhere. I don't even know if he's still out there or if—"

The words failed her, and I saw the tears welling. I felt a very male indecision, to comfort the crying woman or to leave her alone.

I chose the safe option and sipped my coffee.

"How about your husband? How's he handling it?"

"Mike? I—He's hurt, I suppose, yes. He doesn't show it enough, but it's there."

I felt something nagging at the back of my mind again, the way it had when I met them in the pub.

"Is it affecting your relationship? The two of you?"

She laughed, and the tears were gone in an instant. The defensive wall had appeared again.

"No, it's not going to split us up."

"Mrs. Perry—"

"Steph."

"Steph. Is there anything you didn't want to tell me in front of your husband yesterday? I sensed tension between you two."

"Isn't there always tension between parents?"

I let it go at that.

"And you really can't think of anything that would make Chris run away? Anything he'd be particularly upset about?"

"He'd seemed happier lately, more sure of himself. I can't think of anyone less likely to run away."

"He had an appointment with his university mentor last Thursday. Do you have any idea what it could have been about?"

"No. Aren't you going to ask his mentor?"

"Yes, I'll be seeing him again to go over the details."

"Again? So you've already talked to him? Is he the one who said I was lying?"

"No, nobody questioned what you've said. I didn't mean to imply they had. It's just different people's impressions of your son seem to be different."

"Sorry."

"What time will your husband be home from work?"

"Oh, I don't know. He could be a while yet."

"Well, I can catch him another time. I'll call ahead next time so that you both know I'm coming." I smiled. "Have you got the details of Chris's friends?"

"Yes." She beamed. "I wrote it all down."

She rummaged in her bag and handed me a sheet of paper with names and phone numbers.

"This will be a great help," I assured her. "Honestly, I think Chris is OK. And I'm going to find him."

I felt sorry for her, trying not to show how upset she was, but there was still something that didn't sit right.

Something I couldn't place.

I don't really follow a logical progression for finding people. I just nag away at it the way you work a Magic Eye puzzle. Stare at the problem long enough, and the answer pops out. Another piece of the puzzle that was nagging at me was something I caught her with just before I left.

"How about Michael's political stuff? Is that causing any problems?"

She didn't answer, just shrugged. That seemed to convey a lot more than any white lie or platitude would have done. There was something there, and I knew I was looking right at it.

NINETEEN

I parked outside my mother's house. I didn't go in straight-away. Something kept me in the car for a long time. Her cat, Rollo, sat on the wall beside the car and stared at me. It became a brief battle of wills. He didn't invite me in and I didn't run him over. I climbed out of the car and rang the front doorbell. Mum answered pretty much straightaway. She tried to hide the surprise on her face, covering it with happiness. She pulled me into a hug as I stepped through the door and did that thing where you get kissed on the cheek whether you like it or not.

I followed her into the living room, and she motioned for me to sit on the sofa after she cleared away some newspaper. She disappeared into the kitchen, and I heard the kettle boiling. I sat alone, staring at the photographs on the wall.

Me, my brother, and sister.

Family memories.

Strangers.

There was a photo of me and my father in front of a *vardo*, a traditional Gypsy wagon, grinning like fools. I'd never actually seen anyone living in one of those, but some families had them as showpieces. The smiles in the photo held my attention, the same grin on faces separated by age. I tried to remember the last time I'd seen that smile on either of us, but it just drifted into the last time I'd seen him, the time he'd called me a failure. I thought of the last time I'd seen my brother, his arm pressed into my throat, his mouth saying he was going to kill me.

Mum handed me a mug of warm tea and sat opposite me. Born and raised in the area, she still carried the warmth of her Irish grandparents. It made her open and caring, always seeming full of love and life. She was all the things I was not.

"How long's it been, Eoin?"

I shrugged. "Don't know."

Her eyes dimmed a little, and that made the lines around them show up. My mum was in her fifties, and healthy for it, but she looked old when she worried.

She peered at me over her cup. "Are you feeling any better?"

"Better? What do you mean?"

"Well, have you spoken to, what's his name, that Scottish psychia—"

"Dr. Guthrie, no."

She paused, then shrugged, as everyone did when they hit my brick wall. "Good to see you, anyway."

"Do you remember a local couple, used to drink in the pub, the Perrys?"

It took a second to register, and then the dimness in her eyes turned to something hard and cold.

"Oh," she said, "you're running one of your errands. Who's it for this time, those Asian guys?"

"It's not like that."

She just shook her head and looked at me as though I'd killed the cat.

"Sorry, *Mei*. It's just something important I'm working on, that's all. I need to find out what they were like, what they *are* like."

She nodded and played along, but the warmth didn't come back to her voice.

"The Perrys, you said? Name rings a bell."

I described them, and she nodded.

"Yes. I know who you mean now. Steph and, what was his name, Mick? Mark? The copper, that's what I remember. Your dad never trusted him. Well, you know what he thought of the police."

Only too well.

"They were regulars for a while. Strange couple. She was always really nice, got involved, you know? Always asking if she could help arrange quizzes and things like that. But him? Not a bit of it. Always seemed uncomfortable."

"Why, was there anything about him that stood out, anything to make you worry about him?"

"Worry? No. We just wrote him off as a cop, you know? He thought he was above us or something. But then, most of the town did too. Nothing strange about him that way."

"When did they stop coming in?"

"Well, I think he started drinking somewhere else. The Spring Tavern or something, if I remember what your dad said. She kept coming in for a while after that, but they had a son to look after, and I guess she drew the short straw."

"The Spring? Isn't that the Coley pub?"

The Coley family were another with a bad reputation like ours. I don't know if theirs was any more or less earned. They'd been a family of Gypsies who'd settled down between the world wars, so they were firmly established as locals by the time I was born. They had the usual rumors that followed them around—criminal activities like theft and poaching. My dad had always told me never to believe any of it, that it was racist bullshit. But he'd still always told me not to associate with them. My brother had fallen in with them for a time before he left town, one of the many cracks in our family's relationships.

What did it mean if Perry had fallen in with them too? Was that one of the things he wanted to keep locked away in the closet?

"Did he seem honest? I mean, would he have been on the take from the Coleys?"

"All cops are on the take, right?"

The look in her eyes bored into my soul. I left it at that. I gave her a frosty hug at the front door. She didn't say it had been wonderful. She didn't tell me to come again soon. The cat came to laugh me away at the car.

I drove back to my house through habit.

I stood in the driveway. I lost track of how long I was there, staring in through the windows of my own house. I just kept picturing the photographs on my mum's wall. Family life. The past. A lie.

I got back in the car and drove to the flat. I sat down in the darkness broken by the television. I felt alone, but it didn't feel bad. The bottle of whiskey I'd bought a few nights ago was still mostly full, and I sat with it keeping me warm. An old black-and-white film was playing on the TV, which got me thinking about the hooker I'd slept with and our conversation about the old femme fatales. My thoughts drifted to Bauser and Chris and then settled on Mary for a long time.

I watched a few repeated BBC comedies before making my way to the bedroom. The bottle was light in my hand, and I noticed just how much I'd drunk. The bottle had about a third left in it, sloshing about at the bottom, begging to be finished.

The drink can creep up on you if you're not careful. I slipped off my clothes and climbed into bed. Lying there in the dark, I was haunted by a strange feeling, a cold rush up my spine. I switched the bedside lamp on.

Mary was sitting on the bed next to me. Not saying a word.

I looked away.

"Go away," I said. "You're not really here. I'm drunk."

When I steeled myself to look again, she had gone.

TWENTY

Dreams.

Dreams don't like me.

My dreams were full of Mary, as I had met her, drunk and moody, as I had imagined her last night, angry with me, lonely. Chris Perry kept finding his way into the narratives. All I had to form him were a photograph and other people's opinions. Other people's lies. Then I was in either the Myvod or Posada, being laughed at by the locals. They pointed and called me names; they asked where my caravan was. And Bauser kept sitting next to me, getting in the way, asking for drinks and attention. Freud would have had a field day, I suppose.

Then the scene shifted again, and I was in my police uniform. I woke covered in sweat, feeling groggy.

It was eight o'clock in the morning. The bottle of whiskey was on my bedside table. I put it in the drawer, unable to face it. I decided drink wasn't worth the dreams it gave me. A low buzzing nagged at me, as if my headache was actually producing noise. It took me over a minute to figure out that the buzzing was actually my new phone, lost in the pile of my clothes. I fished it out and answered it.

"Get up," said Becker.

"How did you get this number?"

"You called me from it, remember? Phones can do this remarkable thing where they remember numbers."

I rubbed the bridge of my nose. The hangover was fighting at the edges of my vision, deciding whether to go for it full blast or slink away in defeat.

"Yeah, OK. I remember."

"You sound a little rusty. Rough night?"

"Strange dreams."

"OK, well, listen, get a shower and a suit. I'll be round in an hour."

"Wait, wha—?"

"Bauser's funeral today. I thought I should go, and I know you should."

I didn't know if I had the courage to face it. But he was right. I got the kid killed; the least I could do was show my face at his send-off. Bauser had a big family. I remembered them from years ago. Could I face them?

"You're at home, right?"

"Uh." I didn't really want to tell him I wasn't. That would lead to questions. Plus my suit was at the house. "Yeah, I'll see you in an hour."

"Less than that now. Get moving."

Fifty minutes later I was sitting on the front doorstep of my house.

My suit was clean, untouched in the last year, and my tie was as close to correct as I would ever get it.

Becker pulled up and tooted his horn. The toot was totally unnecessary, since I was waiting for him, but it was something he'd always done since we first became friends. Back then we'd be heading out for actual fun. Dinner out, drinks at the pub. We both knew today would be the opposite of fun, but old rituals die hard.

He was driving some kind of family estate car without the family in it. There was an empty crisp packet on the seat as I climbed in and some mainstream country played on his CD deck.

"Like it?" He grinned at me as I stared at the CD cover.

"No."

I strapped in and closed my eyes, hoping we could drive in silence. The hangover had been steadily building for the past hour. It was a stealth hangover, one that bides its time. Being in a moving car was actually a relief; the motion canceled out the world moving around me.

Becker wasn't going to let me have silence, though.

"You cracked the case yet?"

"No. Sorry. Just finding more questions."

He grinned. He looked like a child who just found free porn.

"What's so funny?"

"I knew it. You'll never change, Eoin."

"Don't know what you mean."

"Yes, you do. You get a hold of something, and you never let go. Like a dog or a boy scout or some mutant mix of both."

"I just don't like mysteries. They piss me off."

"So the boy's as good as found."

"I think at least one person I've spoken to already knows where he is."

"The father?"

"No. The lecturer. The father knows more than he's saying, but I get the feeling that Paul Lucas knows what's happened."

"Interesting—"

"No, you had your shot at this. Leave it to me. I need the money, and you've got a pensioner on death's door."

"No, she's off the critical list. She's doing OK. She's not ready to talk yet, but she will be soon, and she'll be able to identify the attacker."

"A happy ending?"

"No. She's got a broken hip, she'll never walk right again, and I think she'll be too scared to leave her home from this point on. It's terrible."

"But the press will make you look good."

"Yes."

"So, a happy ending."

"Very much so."

His smile turned cruel, but honest.

"And the stuff I asked you to look into?"

"Uh huh. Like I said before, you do this thing with the missing student, then you get your information. You always worked best with a carrot on a stick."

"Look, Beck, this is important. OK?"

"So's the student. Do your dog-with-a-bone thing one bone at a time," he said.

I was too tired and hungover to argue.

"Perry said something interesting when I met him," I said. "He said he had enemies—on the force, I mean. You know anything about this?"

"It's a job, you know how it is. Everyone has enemies in every job. All that politics, the bitching, especially when you're brass like him."

"No, it was the way he said it. Like, I'd asked him why not just report his son missing to you guys officially, do it the right way, and he said that about enemies. Is there anyone on the force he might be scared of?"

"You mean could someone on the job be involved?" He looked over at me. I didn't need to answer. "Look, I've not given you this to rock the boat. Don't do anything that'll blow back on me, please? Besides"—he paused while he changed gear—"that kind of thing would be above my pay grade."

We pulled into Bushbury Crematorium just before the funeral procession arrived. It was a modest line of traffic, the hearse followed by five or six cars. My breath caught when I saw the coffin in the back of the hearse. It had flowers alongside arranged to look like a sports car, and another set of flowers in the window spelled out the word "son."

I recognized Bauser's mother as she climbed out of the limousine. I'd actually quite fancied her a few years back when I met her. She'd been young and strong looking, ready to shout me down as a copper and take on the whole force in the name of defending her boy.

Now she looked broken and old. With her was an elderly lady who I guessed must be the grandmother. I remembered that she'd been a child who'd come across on the *Windrush*, one of a boatload of immigrants looking for the promised land. She held the hand of Bauser's younger brother, Marcus. Out of the following cars climbed the rest of the family, the aunts and uncles, their children in suits too big for them, playing adults on their cousin's big day. They all huddled protectively round Bauser's mother as they filed into the hall.

I didn't think I was going to be able to go through with it—until I saw that Laura had come. She was representing the force, I guess. If she was going to do it, then I was going to do it. She nodded at me as she walked past, a slight smile at the edge of her mouth. I caught her perfume, and it cut against her formal appearance. It smelled like liquid gold.

Finally, before Becker and I made our way inside, a minibus pulled up. The Mann brothers had taken the tactful option of not showing up, but they had sent their lieutenants to pay their respects. They filed out of the minibus and formed a somber queue, following us in.

The service was muted. The priest said a few respectful words, and one of Bauser's uncles led us all in a gospel hymn. For a moment I almost felt spiritual, feeling the tug of the words, touching on the old-time religion of my father's family. After that and another speech from the priest, one of the children gave a speech that he'd written himself. It was all about his big cousin Eric and how he was happy now in heaven. I couldn't breathe. I only stopped from crying by zoning out, thinking of a suitable soundtrack for the funeral.

The coffin disappeared behind a curtain, and that was it. The last journey finished.

Everyone stood and filed out through a door at the front, waiting in a queue to say some pleasantries to the family. Ahead of me, I saw Laura having a long conversation with Bauser's mother and grandmother. She looked good. She looked strong. She looked every bit the leader and states-man, and I realized she was destined for her job.

When it was my turn to speak, Bauser's mother took my hands in hers and squeezed.

"The Gypsy man," she said. "I remember you. Eric said you always had time for him. That meant a lot to him—and me."

I choked again, and this time my eyes welled up. "I'm sorry" were the only words I could manage before shuffling off to find Becker's car.

Laura waved at us as we pulled away.

I grimaced and nodded but didn't wave back. I wasn't feeling particularly gracious at that point.

"Looks good in that uniform, doesn't she?" Becker had just enough of a leer to his voice to make my stomach jump.

"I should be proud of her, I suppose."

"You getting a nostalgic feeling?"

"No."

He mulled something over, then shrugged. "She told me you're not talking to the doctor she sorted out for you."

"No."

"He's not going to chase after you forever, you know."

"Good."

"I don't get you, man. I never really did, but these couple of years? You've just stopped. Maybe no one else cares enough about you to tell you straight, but Eoin, you're fucking up."

Was this what my mum had held back from saying?

"Leave it, Beck. Would you rather I followed your route and stayed with the force simply because I had nothing better to do? Stayed with Laura simply because I had nobody else to go to? Is that what you think I should be doing?"

"You used to be a part of life. You've drifted out to the edge of somewhere, and you don't seem to care."

"Never go back. The past is the past. Never go back, and that's it."

"Now you're just putting up excuses. You're good at it, though. Almost as good as you are at taking money from the Mann brothers."

"Oh, fuck off. Get out of my head."

We drove the rest of the way back in silence. The only sound came when I slammed the door shut behind me when we got to my house. He pulled away without a word.

He didn't toot the horn.

TWENTY-ONE

I'd hit a brick wall in the shape of Becker. He wasn't going to play ball until I'd finished his job for him, the lazy fucker. But he was right. And as I'd watched Bauser's coffin glide behind the curtain, I'd felt the pain of a family being split up. I had the idea I wasn't going to let that happen again. I was going to find Chris and find him fast.

I drove back to my hometown and headed straight for the Spring Tavern. At one time it had been the only pub on a busy stretch of road, a bridge that led to the next town over. It had been a stopping point for truck drivers and tourists and a liquor trap for local teenagers. But then the bridge had been demolished as a new road was built, one that cut out the need for drivers ever to come this way. It became a dead end, and the pub became a regular spot only for those with reason to be there or no reason to be anywhere else.

It was a freestanding building with a huge concrete yard at the back, which had once been the layover point for the trucks. Now it was just a graveyard for rusted cars and a toilet for the local dogs. The pub was still organized the right way, split into a lounge bar and a public bar. The public side would be deserted at this time of day; the regulars would still be at work or collecting their dole money. I walked into the lounge and took a look around me.

The decor was older than me, cream wallpaper that had yellowed with age. At head height the wall was marked with tobacco stains, where generations of smoke had hung in the air. The carpet was a well-worn brown pattern that had turned shiny and black in the most trodden areas. The seats were wooden benches that ran along the walls, and the tables looked like freshly varnished driftwood.

Ash Coley was seated at the far end of the bar, farthest away from me. Three of his biggest hangers-on were with him, playing cards and sucking on cigarettes as though there wasn't a smoking ban in place. Ash was the head of the family these days, after his father had been killed in a Birmingham street brawl a few years previously. He was about ten years older than me and quite a bit wider. His chin had spread downward beneath a strong jaw line, merging with his neck to make him look like a walrus in a T-shirt.

"Well, it's the Miller kid," he called over at me after eyeing me up. "You come to pay your brother's debt?"

I shook my head.

"To apologize for your daddy, then? God knows, somebody should."

"No."

"What then, sunshine? You know you're not welcome in here."

What the hell. Why play it safe?

"What's between you and Michael Perry?"

His eyes narrowed, and he spread his hands out, laying them palm down on the table. That seemed to be some sort of signal, because his three stooges stood up and made a couple of steps toward me. I felt fresh air on the back of my neck as someone stepped in behind me. I didn't turn to look who it was, not wanting to take my eyes off the trouble in front of me, but I heard the bolt slam home on the door after it shut.

Locked in.

On the plus side, it looked as though my instincts were right. There was something deeper here to scratch at.

Whoever was behind me pushed forward once, twice. On the third push I got the message and walked over to Coley's table. I turned then to see who had been pushing me, and it was a small, squirrel-like guy, wiry and frayed looking with a knife in his left hand.

Ash's eyes were cold and heavy.

"You come in here, *Diddikai*, and start making demands? That *chora* father of yours taught you no manners, eh?"

So I was a half-blood and my father was a thief. Nice. There's nothing like a warm welcome.

I shot back. "So you *do* know Perry, then?"

Coley flicked his head to one side, and the stooge nearest to me punched me in the kidneys. I doubled over and almost fell to my knees, but managed to stay on my feet out of stubbornness. That, or the fact that two of the other stooges were holding me up.

"Let's try this again, shall we? Now, you're a guest here. See how we're making you welcome? How about you ask nicely?"

"I've heard that Michael Perry used to drink in here. Is that right?"

"He did, yes. For a while."

"His son has gone missing. Do you know anything about it?"

I felt rather than saw the stooge behind me raise his fist. But Coley shook his head a little and then motioned for me to sit in the chair in front of him. He waved and shouted for someone to fetch me a drink, and an ice-cold bottled beer was put on the table in front of me. Coley then leaned back and eyed me up and down again.

"So, Mickey's son has run away, right?"

I'd never heard anyone use that nickname for Michael.

"What makes you say he's run away?"

"Had to happen at some point. That whole family are running from one thing or another. Just like yours, I reckon."

I ignored that last bit and sipped at the drink. My moral high ground was not above accepting gifts. "What do you mean? What are they running from?"

"Not my place to say. Mick's got a few things hidden away; you'd need to ask him what they were."

There was something in the way he said it. As though he would have told me if his stooges weren't around. I wondered what could be so secret that he wouldn't tell me in front of the hired help.

"So you're friends?"

"I wouldn't say *friends*. I don't think he has any, not really. But he used to come round here while it served him."

"Doesn't sound like a good memory."

"He liked being here until it became inconvenient. As soon as it was embarrassing, we were old news."

"Who did he replace you with, any ideas?"

"Just a better class of people. Suits and ties. Handshakes. The right *kind* of handshakes, if you know what I mean."

"Bribes?"

He sipped his own drink and then shook his head. "Like I said, you need to ask him. But he's going into politics, right? Not a cheap game, that. A man from around here, he'd need some help."

"So you're saying he's bent."

There was a twinkle in his eye. He nodded at the stooges and they stood back, the tension in the room fading away.

"Good luck finding the boy. I hope he's well."

I knew enough to quit and stood, nodding at Coley and turning to leave. The squirrel guy stepped forward and punched me in the gut, and this time I did hit the floor. One of the bigger guys then kicked me hard in the face, and the room spun around me. As it slowed down I heard Coley laugh.

"Just a friendly reminder," he said, "you come in here again, and we won't be so nice."

TWENTY-TWO

Coley's words hung in my mind. Was Perry on the take? Was someone sponsoring his ambitions? I would have no idea where to start with that. The world of money, secret meetings, and politics was a scary place. I needed to get back into the world I *did* know.

I drove into Wolverhampton and walked onto the university campus without any security guards stopping me.

I began asking round campus. I had the names of Chris's friends. They had to be there somewhere. I wasn't getting any helpful answers. In the canteen I tried a new trick; I ran through the list of phone numbers that Stephanie had given me. Most of them went to voicemail, but finally one began to ring. I saw a young woman at a table in the corner pull her phone out of her bag and stare at the number. She shook her head and canceled the call. The phone in my hand disconnected.

I tried my best smile as I walked over and introduced myself. Three of them were sitting at the table. The leader of the group, a woman in her early twenties who looked slightly older than the others, was named Kelly. She wore a red scarf around her neck and seemed to view herself as an actor with a capital *A*. It was her phone that I'd rung. As she looked me up and down, I realized I was still in my suit from

the funeral, and she seemed to assume I was a cop. Either
that or she just liked talking to anyone who'd listen.

"Chris was fun," she told me. "He loved to go out. We
went clubbing a few times in the first semester, us and a
few other people who were on the course at that point, and
Chris stood out."

"In what way?"

"Well, to talk to him, like normally, as if he was sat here
with us now, he was shy. But get him in a club, and he was
different. Life and soul, y'know?"

"So he liked to party?"

"Oh, yes. He was better at that than anything else. He
wasn't an actor, not really."

"He liked drink, did he, at these parties?"

"Oh, yes."

"That's funny," cut in someone else at the table, a young-
looking male. "I never saw Chris drink."

I turned my attention to him. His name was Ryan, and
he was a year below the others.

"What did you think of Chris?"

"He was a laugh. He was very quiet, not loud or noticeable, but he had a great sense of humor. He was one of the
few people you'd meet here who seemed sure of themselves.
He had a grip on who he was."

There was a heaviness to his words. I wondered if he was
making a point to someone else at the table.

"I don't know," said Kelly. "Maybe he just paid attention when we were taught about acting. He definitely had a
broody streak in him."

"When was the last time you saw him?"

They all exchanged looks, trying to figure it out, or trying to get their answers straight.

"Last Tuesday," Kelly said. "I'm sure it was last
Tuesday."

"A couple of weeks ago," Ryan said after much thought. "I haven't seen him lately. I've been behind on my work so I haven't been seeing anyone."

I looked at the redheaded boy named Mark, but he wasn't looking at me. He was staring off into the middle distance, ignoring the whole conversation.

I leaned forward.

"Mark?"

"Thursday," he said after a long pause. "I saw him on Thursday."

"That's the last day anyone saw him."

"Is it?"

"Yes. You and Paul Lucas are the two people I've found who saw him last."

He just looked at me while I stared back, trying to read his thoughts. I noticed that Kelly and Ryan were staring at him as well. I knew Kelly and Ryan were being straight. It was written on their faces that they were telling the truth. I'd never met a drama student good enough to hide that. But Mark knew something. Was it the same secret Paul Lucas was holding back?

I took my thoughts up to Lucas's office.

I looked in through the thin vertical window set into the doorframe and saw that he was with a student. I moved away from the door so he wouldn't notice me and leaned against the opposite wall.

I waited for fifteen minutes before the door opened and the student shuffled past me with a ring binder full of paperwork. I knocked once and then walked in without waiting for an answer. Lucas didn't smile when he saw me.

"You should have made an appointment," he said.

"I can see that you're very busy," I said. I smiled and sat down. "I've found that two people saw Chris last Thursday.

For all intents and purposes, we'll call that the day he disappeared, shall we?"

He gave the smallest shuffle of his head, a gesture that was neither a nod nor a shrug.

"Two people, that's all. One of them was you."

I leaned back, making myself comfortable. I'd noticed that the more liberties I took, the more pissed off he got. I liked that.

"You saw him on the day he disappeared. So what was your meeting about?"

"Nothing important. I'm tutoring him through his third-year project. I was checking his progress."

"What is his project?"

"It's a script. He's writing a script. Then he was going to produce a one-off performance of it and write an essay evaluating it all."

"Can I see it?"

"What?"

"His script. I presume he was getting close to finishing it by now?"

"Pretty much, all but the final scene."

"So can I?"

"No, of course not. It's private. I can't, and won't, show you his project any more than I would show you anyone else's."

"Mr. Lucas, I'm not interested in anyone else. I'm interested in Chris."

"Look, I understand, but I absolutely can't let you read a student's work. It would be against the rules, and frankly, it would be just wrong."

"You're either holding out on something or you're lying. I just don't know which. But I will."

He shook his head. "I'm sorry, I don't—"

"What was his script about?"

He blinked, caught off guard.

"Alcohol," he said. "A young man and alcohol."

"Mr. Lucas, was Chris an alcoholic?"

"No."

He said it firmly, meeting my eyes dead-on.

I left without saying anything further. I didn't need anything more from him. I was back out in the courtyard, walking toward the main entrance, when I heard someone call me.

I turned to see Mark, the red-haired student from the canteen, walking fast to catch up with me.

"Was Chris an alcoholic?" I called out, probably too loud.

It was a hell of a greeting, but it was the best I was going to give.

"Yes." He said it quietly. No fuss.

"Let's talk," I said.

TWENTY-THREE

We crossed the road to Jay's Café.

It was a small greasy spoon. It only survived during weekdays on students and police officers. On weekends it bustled with football fans.

We sat down at a table at the back. I had a glass of Coke, and Mark had a black coffee.

"Tell me about him" was all it took.

"Chris was great," Mark said with a smile. "First year, get a drink in him, he really was the life and soul of the party. Well, that's how it looked. You had to get to know him. Even at the parties there was a sadness in him. He really beat himself up about something, but none of us ever found out what it was."

"So he was prone to depression."

"Oh, yes. Lots of it."

I guess I wasn't too surprised to hear that. Chris's mother had told me that he definitely wasn't depressed, but then, mothers aren't the most reliable reporters.

"He just had a way of melting into the background," Mark said. "Like he didn't want to be seen. You could sit at a crowded table for half an hour before realizing Chris was there."

"Total opposite of his other face."

"Yes, the drink did that, does that."

I noticed that he changed from past tense to present, and his tone of voice changed too, turned lower, more serious.

"But what everybody's been telling me is that he's changed this year?"

"Yes. He realized what his problems were, the ones we know about and the ones we don't. He just seemed to face up to them."

"The alcohol."

"You want the truth? I'm not even sure he's really an alcoholic. I mean, yes, he drank to solve problems. But deep down, I don't think he's an alcoholic in the same way the other people you meet are. I think he just found that idea as a good way to, I don't know—"

"To give a name to his problems."

"Does that make sense?"

"Yes, I guess it does," I said.

"Well, whatever, it helped. He was full of confidence this year. Like he'd figured out who he was and what he wanted to do, and quitting drinking was a big part of that."

"You quit with him?"

"What makes you say that?"

"Well, a few minutes ago, you said something that made me think you were talking about yourself as well as Chris, and then when you said—"

"When I said 'the other people you meet.'"

"Yes." He paused and took a long sip of his coffee.

I've met a couple of recovering alcoholics over the years, and there's something in their stare, something in its frank honesty, that unsettles me.

"Well, you're right. I am. Alcoholic, I mean. And I really am. I just love the drink. Some people don't understand how you can drink so much, but they don't get it. I just don't understand, I can't understand, how people can stop at one."

I nodded.

I've never known what to say to confessions like this. I just nod.

"And Chris got me into the program."

"Program?"

"AA. Alcoholics Anonymous."

"There's one around here?"

"Of course. They're everywhere if you look. There's one at the university. That's more like an overblown support group than proper AA. And there's a place just down the road where there are three, sometimes four AA meetings a week."

"How many do you go to?"

"As many as I can. Sometimes all of them."

"Chris?"

"He went to a couple a week. It seemed to get him by."

"Anybody there get to really know him?"

"Listen, I can't do this. We don't share our secrets, other people's secrets, to those outside the group."

"But you've already told me—"

"Too much. I've already told you too much. I feel like I've already cheated everyone in the group, but the trade-off is I've given you some information about Chris that you wouldn't get from his friends or family. I can't give you any more. But usually, if someone stops turning up to AA, if an alcoholic goes missing, it means one of two things."

"Which are?"

"He's either dead or he's propped up in a pub some-where. And neither one of those is good. That's why Paul Lucas is covering for Chris."

"What's Lucas got to do with any of this?"

"He's Chris's sponsor."

Boom.

Of course Chris was an alcoholic. That had been obvious from the start. I just hadn't seen it until today.

And now I knew why Lucas was covering it up. Not just to protect Chris—that was a best-case scenario for his motives. No, he was protecting himself. Addiction was part of modern life. Even on the force, there had been programs in place to offer help to employees who came forward. I bet every HR department in the country would go to lengths to claim there was no stigma involved. But the media deals in witch hunts and moral panics, not reason and modernity. If a senior and respected tutor at the city's only university was shown to be sponsoring students into AA, his career wouldn't survive the explosion.

I thanked Mark, paid for the drinks, and left him to his sobriety.

My next impulse, naturally, was to head to the pub.

I didn't want a drink. I'd promised myself I wouldn't. But I wanted to sit in the pub, on my usual stool, and stop thinking for a while.

One of the windows at Posada was covered with a large piece of cardboard, the glass smashed to a jagged edge. Brown parcel tape held the cardboard in place. There'd been a break-in and the pub was full of outraged drunks no longer feeling that their bar was their castle.

"Anything taken?" I asked the landlord.

"Just two bottles of leap frog. The till was empty."

I ordered a Coke and sat staring into it.

Chris was an alcoholic. I needed to attend a meeting. He might be there. Or someone there might know where he was. I pushed off the stool and headed back out.

As I stood outside the pub trying to decide which direction to turn, a car pulled up by the curb beside me. Then there was a strong grip on my arm, and I found myself being pushed down into the car by Bull. He slid in beside me without a word, and we pulled back out into traffic. I wasn't in the mood to talk. I just sat in a sulk, staring out the window.

We crossed the ring road and headed past the football ground into Whitmore Reans. It was an area with an identity crisis. Long tagged as one of the problem spots of the city, it had seen a lot of cash pumped in over the past twenty years. Some of the problems moved away to other areas. Others just took firmer hold.

After a couple of minutes, we pulled onto the car park of a new sports hall. It was the size of a school gym, and from inside came the sounds of a football match: Shouting. Swearing. Squeaking trainers.

Bull got out of the car and pulled me after him. He led me through a small reception area and into the hall. The game was in full flow, teenagers running back and forth, sweating and sliding. A coach was running around with them, shouting out encouragement and refereeing.

At the top of a small flight of stairs was the spectators' area, plastic chairs lined up for an imaginary crowd and a solitary vending machine in the corner. Veronica Gaines was waiting there, wrapped up in a dark coat. I rubbed my arm when Bull released his grip. There was going to be a bruise to match my growing collection.

"You couldn't just ask politely? You had to try and make me cry?"

The brute almost smiled.

"All part of his dry wit," Veronica said.

"You like that line," I said.

She looked me up and down. I probably looked tired and beat up.

"How far have you gotten on our little project?"

"I'm close," I said. "I just need to know the right questions to ask to the right people."

"That doesn't sound any closer than the last time we spoke."

"You'd be surprised. I know I usually am."

"Well, I'm glad you haven't wasted too much time on it."

"No, I'm serious. I'm almost there."

"I'm serious too. I want you to stop."

I was lost for words. I wasn't very proud of it. I stood there for a moment, rubbing my arm and probably looking puzzled.

"You want me to stop?"

"Yes. I want you to leave the whole thing alone."

"What's changed since last time?"

She smiled. She tilted her head to one side and watched the game for a moment. It was almost as though she'd been told not to look me in the eye when lying to me.

"Things have changed. That's all."

"But you've paid me."

"Keep it. Think of it as a retainer."

"A retainer for what?"

"Look at them, running around. Working harder than at any job they've tried to hold down."

"What is this place?"

"One of my projects. Well, my father's really, but I've taken to it myself."

"You built this place?"

"Built it, opened it, paid for the coach. Those kids haven't had to pay a penny. They just have to keep turning up."

"And what, you get them hooked young?"

She shot me a hard glance. "We have rules here. Any of them found high, even once, they're out. No drugs in here."

"How noble," I said.

How confusing, I thought.

"Recognize any of them?"

I took a look, focusing on the faces, the body language, the way they spoke.

"The one in goal? I think I arrested his big brother a few years back."

"You did. Auto theft and possession. He's still inside."

"And the kid on the ball now, with the lousy left foot? I caught him stealing from the Mann brothers last year, gave him a cuff and sent him running."

"So you didn't tell the brothers?"

"God no, they'd break his legs."

She smiled to herself and nodded. Then she turned and shared the smile with me.

"I was right about you. This is what you should be doing. You like giving kids a second chance, not locking them up. Come and work here instead. We could do with another coach."

"And what, be part of your noble second chance program? Social work funded by drugs?"

"Do you see the government down here? The council? All they do is sell off the land to housing companies and car showrooms. Good teams like the Wolves and Albion have sent scouts, though, and Villa too. Wolves players even volunteer, come and give talks. These kids can get noticed in here. But take a look at them, what don't you see?"

I looked again. There were white kids and black kids, working up a sweat and sharing jokes.

"No Asians."

She nodded. "But you walk outside, onto the estates, and they're all over. It's like Little India out there. So what's going on?"

"Actually most of them are from—"

She killed my sentence with a look, so I changed tack. "Well, it's not as though there're many Asian footballers to inspire them over here."

"Come on. You know we could get them in here. If the Mann brothers weren't trying to sew things up so tight, we could get Asians in here just like any others. You could do that. You could break the cliques."

Right. So that's what it was. Turf warfare through charity work.

"You just want into that market. You just want me to bring more business into your hands."

"I'm sorry you think so badly of me. Trust me, Eoin, if I wanted you to bring us more Asian business, I would ask you. I'm just trying to give you a job that fits. One that uses you better than the police ever did, better than the brothers do. Away from the drugs and gangs. Working with people. Think it over. And one more thing? I'm serious about the case. Drop it. Stay away from the Polish guy, and stay away from the Mann wankers."

I was getting warned away a lot. Laura wanted me to stay away from the Mann brothers. Gaines wanted me to stay away from the Mann brothers and the Polish guy.

Only days ago, Veronica had been throwing me money to look into it for her. She had found something in the meantime that she wanted me away from. I filed that away to use later. Right now I was thinking of my conversation with Coley, of a subject that Gaines would know about.

"Listen, if I was looking to find someone around here who would bribe politicians, who would I look for?"

She smiled. "Me."

"Do you know Michael Perry?"

"I hear his son is missing."

"How do you know that?"

"It's my job to know." She smiled at me and blew a kiss before walking away down the steps. I made to follow, but Bull raised his hand. I flinched.

"I guess I'm not invited," I said.

Bull nodded and followed Gaines.

TWENTY-FOUR

The autumn day, full of half-gray dusky light, had died.

The muted sun was setting as I walked back to the house, where I'd left the car that morning. The funeral felt like a long time ago, but I wanted to change my clothes and see if I could stomach staying in the house again.

I put my keys in the door but hesitated and looked up at the house. I couldn't keep avoiding it. I opened the front door and let it swing in away from me. The smell of fresh paint and disinfectant greeted me, and I remembered that Bobby had been working on the place. I began walking from room to room, switching on the lights. The walls gleamed with fresh pastel-colored paint. The hardwood floors shone. There was a brand new fitted kitchen, and the fridge had been restocked.

Upstairs, the bathroom was fixed and polished, and my bedroom had a fresh set of paint and furniture. This had cost far more than I'd given Bobby, and I guessed it was another favor from the Mann brothers. The new bed was huge and looked like the most comfortable thing I'd ever seen.

The doorbell sounded, and it was a new sound.

I had to laugh. Bobby had even replaced my doorbell.

I don't know who I expected as I opened the door, but it wasn't Laura.

She stood there, still in her suit, looking tired. There was drink on her breath, and for the first time I noticed a little bit of age around her eyes. My heart did something it hadn't done for a few years, and I stepped aside for her to enter.

She didn't step in, though. She leaned against the door-frame and smiled at me.

"You looked good today," she said.

I didn't answer.

I could have told her how good she'd looked. I could have told her how I thought she looked a little better right now with a few cracks of humanity showing through.

She reached up to touch my face, tracing the edges of the bruise I'd picked up from visiting Ash Coley. "What happened to you?"

She'd broken the silence. I could have counted that as a victory for me, but I didn't feel like keeping score. I didn't feel like playing any games at all.

"What happened to us?" she said.

"I wish I knew," I said. "Want a coffee?"

I stepped farther away from the door, and she followed me in. I made us both coffee and started frying some bacon. She took off her jacket and leaned against the kitchen counter, watching me.

"Place looks good."

"Yeah. I got a friend to fix it up for me. It was looking a little rough."

"Like the two of us."

"No." I held her gaze for a minute and finally said it. "You look pretty good if you ask me."

She smiled and lowered her head, hiding a blush. Something passed between us that neither of us missed, and I wasn't sure I could cope with where it was heading. I turned away and busied myself with the food, making her a sandwich and turning back to hand it to her.

Our hands touched as I gave her the plate, and I felt it again. There wasn't much time to change direction before we did something stupid.

"Why are you here?"

She put down the plate and looked at me hard for a minute or two. The tiredness was written large across her eyes, but there was loneliness as well. I recognized it from looking in the mirror every morning.

I stepped in and kissed her gently, tasting vodka on her tongue. She stepped into it and kissed harder. The first few years of our relationship came back in one second, everything up until it started to go wrong, and it all felt right again.

She ran her hand through my hair, and I ran mine across her back, and we got lost for a few moments. She pulled out of the embrace, staying close enough for our noses to touch, and we shared deep, heavy breaths for a moment.

"Sorry," I said.

"Me too."

She searched my eyes, and I realized she was looking for some glimmer of hope. I was probably looking for the same.

"I think I'd like to see you later. Maybe eat a proper meal." She pushed the untouched sandwich away with her spare hand. "You know, relax."

I nodded. "Go home and get changed. Think about it. If you still want me to come round, call me in a couple of hours."

She ran her hand across my bruise again and left. I leaned against the counter and put my head in my hands. What the hell were we doing? My gut tightened into a knot and stayed that way.

Long after the sound of the front door closing had bounced around the hallway, I realized I'd heard another sound. The sound of mail falling on the floor again.

I walked into the hallway and froze.

Again there was the usual collection of junk. But nestled in the pile was another brown envelope. This time the question "Where is it?" was written across the front in block capitals. Inside was a photograph of Mary's body. It looked to be in a worse state than when I'd seen it last, lying on my bed. Now her skin was almost translucent white, and her eyes were filmy. She was lying in the boot of a car. Something metallic in the corner of the photo caught my eye. It was the golf club I keep for emergencies. Then I almost threw up because I knew straightaway that it was my car.

Outside I looked around, making sure there was nobody to see me opening the boot. I lifted the lid and stopped breathing.

Mary was in the boot of my car.

She was staring up at me with her dead eyes. Her mouth hung open more than it had before, and her skin was slightly shrunken. She was still wrapped in my bedsheets, which now seemed to be stuck to her.

As soon as my breathing started again, I breathed in the stench. Now that I knew what it was, it was unmistakeable. Once you've tasted it, you're never going to mistake the smell of a corpse for anything else.

Don't panic.

Fuck it.

Panic.

I was done. This was it.

If it wasn't a watertight case before, with her dead in my house and wrapped in my bedsheets, it was cast-iron now that she'd been stagnating in my car. There was no way out of this that didn't leave me royally fucked.

That buzzing I'd experienced when I first found the body, that heavy hum at the base of my skull, came back big time. The blanket wrapped around my brain again, and I felt the world go away.

When it lifted, I was driving.

It took me a bit to realize where I was, driving through my hometown again like a lost child. The buzzing was still holding onto my skull and my ears, blotting out the noises of the traffic around me. I changed direction without understanding where I was going. I was in the outskirts of the town of Dudley before the buzzing faded enough for me to hear my own thoughts. It was then that I understood what I was doing.

I was looking for the old mines.

The Black Country is riddled with them. I remember reading stories of how, up until quite recently, gasses would occasionally escape from the mines, sending spurts of flame shooting up from the ground at night. The locals, poor and superstitious, said it was the devil walking the streets in the darkness.

Almost all the new housing estates were built either on the sites of old factories or old mines, so it was never hard to find an old shaft even if you didn't know exactly where they were. But it was a specific mine I was heading for. Watching over Dudley from atop one of the tallest hills are the ruins of Dudley castle. A zoo inhabits the grounds of the castle, and as a teenager I used to spend evenings there, getting high with my friends as the animals howled in the dark. One of our best discoveries was that the hill was riddled with tunnels and mine shafts. Some of the tunnels were flooded; some were filled with debris from the castle and housing estates. Some contained the rotted carcasses of exotic animals. We used to fancy that they had escaped from the zoo, but I later found out that the staff dumped the bodies there in the days before paperwork and regulations. These tunnels were being lost as the land was sold and built on. The council had recently announced it was going to fill the caverns with concrete for safety reasons. To bury something here was to lose it forever.

I parked the car on an industrial estate that backed onto the castle hill. In the dark, my path lit by the headlights of passing cars, I retraced my teenage steps. The exact spot where I knew the main entrance shaft to be, my old haunt, was now the foundation of a McDonald's drive-thru, and the second entrance I could remember was now underneath a tarmac car park. Tracing my old walk around the hill toward the zoo, I crawled through some bushes that seemed vaguely familiar and found a rusty grill stuck into a bed of crumbling concrete broken into dusty old clumps. I picked up a piece and dropped it through the grill. Almost right away I heard it hit water. The spaces of the grill were just big enough for me to fit my hand through so I gingerly pushed into the darkness. In a moment I was up to my wrist in cold, clammy water. Most important, the water felt still. There was no current here. Either the council had flooded this section of mine, or it had filled naturally, but it seemed now to be an old and stagnant well. When I pulled out my hand, it was coated with a film of scum from the filthy water.

Perfect.

Walking back out, I came out on a dirt track that led back to the road. A damp wooden fence separated the track from the bushes. Most of the wooden strips were missing from where kids must have pulled them loose over the years. A few kicks knocked out a large section of the fence completely, large enough to squeeze my car, and I stood there for ten minutes, checking that nobody was curious about the noises I'd been making.

I brought the car around the hill slowly, letting cars pass me as fast as they liked so that I could have the road to myself for a moment, and it worked. No cars came by as

I turned onto the dirt track and then eased the car through the gap in the fence. The headlights showed boxes, newspapers, and empty bottles pushed against the fence, no doubt once a home.

The newspapers were all several years old. There were no recent feces or rotting food. It looked clear.

I pulled out the golf club. I have never in my life played the sport, and never swung the club in anger, but it's good to have in the boot just in case. Just in case, for example, you need to pry off a rusty grill to an abandoned well. Just in case you should need to hide evidence. The grill came up with few complaints. The concrete must not have been a good mix to start with, and now that it was old, it fell apart like papier-mâché as I applied pressure.

I used a torch rather than risk the cars headlights, lifting the bundle out of the boot and onto the ground and then dragging it in three attempts to the edge of the hole. With one last look around me, I rolled the bedsheet bundle into the hole. It was more than weighty enough with everything in it, but it took a moment before sinking as the water seeped into it, loosening it a bit. It disappeared slowly down into the oily darkness. Horror-film visions plagued me as the bundle sank past my sight, my brain filling in images of the corpse breaking free of the sheets, reaching toward me.

And then I was free.

A wave of nausea passed over me as the realization truly hit me, and I sat in the car for a while, feeling very tired.

I pulled the grate back over the hole and covered it with branches and the remnants of the wino's old home until I could no longer see the metal.

I coasted the car back through the gap with the lights off, took a minute to prop the broken wood back loosely across the gap, which wouldn't last, and then hit the lights and began the drive home.

The tightness in my gut had not faded. Ever since Laura had left to get changed, it had only grown. It felt as if soon I wouldn't be able to breathe.

My appendix had burst when I was twenty-two, and this pain was similar. I took a couple of painkillers, but they didn't help. I took a long shower, trying to wash the dirty water and imaginary blood off my hands. Then I remembered my conversation with Becker that morning and knew what the pain was.

Never go back.

That's what I'd said. The past is the past, and that's it.

I sat damp on the end of the new bed, the towel wrapped around my waist, and waited. Sure enough, my mobile rang, and I recognized the number as Laura's.

She sounded happy as she said hello, and for a moment so was I.

The pain got worse. I breathed hard, feeling the pause build between us. I imagined her heart was doing the same stretching that mine was. I said sorry. I told her that the timing was wrong, that I didn't think we were doing the right thing. I heard the disappointment in her voice as she told me that she understood, that it wasn't a problem. I heard her lie as she said we could do it another time, and I agreed. After I hung up, the tightness that had been wrapped around my insides faded away.

All I was left with was loneliness.

TWENTY-FIVE

I'm back in the private booth at Legs.

Veronica is dancing for me, just as before. This is all about power, but not mine. Her breath on the crotch of my trousers, I lean back against the sofa and take a lord's name in vain. Her hands are stroking my thighs, getting ever closer.

She unbuttons my jeans, and I'm holding my breath. I lose myself as she puts me in her mouth, the warm closing around me, her tongue moving. I have no smart answers, no strength. I'm just desperate for it to continue.

My wife, Laura, is in the room. I hadn't noticed. She strokes my neck and whispers in my ear. I can't make out what she's saying. It sounds like she's taunting me, insulting me. I don't care.

Veronica takes my cock out of her mouth and instead grips it, stroking, getting me close. She flicks her eyebrow and says something that Laura laughs at. They're both taunting me now.

I beg her to continue. To finish me off. Then I'm back in someone's mouth as I come, being sucked and licked, cleaned. I feel alive and drained.

I cry out.

The lights come up, and I'm alone in the room with Chris.
He's wiping his mouth.
He's wiping me off his mouth.

TWENTY-SIX

"My name's Sharon, and I'm an alcoholic."

It was delivered deadpan, devoid of emotion, like a football score. Sharon was the only person standing. The rest of us sat on plastic chairs arranged in a semicircle, like the audience in a bargain-basement amphitheater.

I was attending an AA meeting and trying very hard not to see myself in any of the people around me.

Sharon was in her late forties, maybe early fifties. She was tall for a woman and looked very tired. Tired wasn't the right word; what she looked was *weary*. She told her story in short, clipped tones that got longer and more emotional as she went on. She talked about what she called her "career of drinking."

"Anybody does something for thirty years," she was saying, "they can call it a career."

There were a few nods and a few grunts of agreement. She continued, talking about something she called "maintenance drinking."

"I never really drank much. Not that I noticed, not that anybody noticed. I never went to the pubs or clubs. I never got drunk. I was never sick at parties. My friends? They would drink too much and pass out or get loud and obnoxious. I never did any of that, so why worry, right? But still, twenty-five years had gone by, and I finally realized I'd been having four or five drinks a night, every night, for twenty-five years."

"I hear ya." A black guy sat in the middle of the room. He looked familiar, like I knew his face from the pubs, another one we'd lost. Sharon looked round the room. Looked at me.

"I realized that I needed it. That I'd always needed it. I realized that I'd always need it, whether I wanted it or not."

The black guy murmured his agreement again, and a few others followed along. I stopped concentrating on Sharon and started looking around the room, trying to take in the people. After calling Laura I'd drifted again. One of my mental fogs, but when I'd snapped out of it I'd called the Samaritans to find out where the AA meetings were held in town. I'd been late coming in, the session already underway when I took my seat at the back.

From the backs of people's heads, I noticed one thing:

So young.

There were older people, like Sharon. But so much of the crowd looked young. Twenties. Maybe under twenty-five.

Kids.

Our drug war. Our Recession. Our casualties. Our alcoholics. We're chewing them up and spitting them out young.

Everyone began a polite round of applause. Sharon took a seat at the front near a younger man. He was in his early thirties and looked like a social worker or a PE teacher. He seemed to be chairing the discussion.

The chair told his own story.

"I'll never forget it. For years my eyesight was going. It only bothered me when I was watching the telly. If I was watching a football match, I couldn't read the scores. They were always blurred. I knew I needed an eye test, but I kept putting it off. I didn't want to wear glasses, you know? But then when I stopped drinking, I could read the scores perfectly. I've got twenty-twenty vision. All those years, it was the drink in me."

There was some muted laughter and more heads nodded. Chairs scraped as people began to stand up, to greet one another, and to walk toward the table where coffee and biscuits waited.

I joined everyone else at the table for coffee in a plastic cup and a couple of digestive biscuits. Turning to face the chairs, I noticed that both Paul Lucas and Mark were sitting there, not far from where I had been. They were deep in conversation and staring at me. I smiled my best annoying grin and raised my coffee to them in a silent toast.

"You're new here."

It wasn't a question. I turned to smile at the chairman. He looked a few years older up close, lines around his eyes that hadn't shown up from a distance, a few faint acne pockmarks on his cheeks.

More like a geography teacher, I decided.

"Dave." He offered me his hand in a firm shake.

"Eoin," I said. "I, uh, just found out about this group."

"That's great."

"Yeah, I just want to keep a low profile though, no fuss."

"Oh sure, of course." He smiled. "We all know what it's like that first time. So how long have you been sober?"

I thought back. When had I had my last drink? Was it yesterday? Was I forgetting one I'd had today?

"Just a day," I said. More like hours, I thought.

If he was surprised by the short duration of my sobriety, he didn't show it. They probably got liars in here all the time, looking for free food or warmth.

"Well, that's great," he said.

Very earnest. Everybody here was very earnest.

"Well, I know it's not much."

"No, no, it's always just a day. Yesterday, today, maybe tomorrow, never think beyond that."

I nodded, hoping I looked like I was taking in his advice. "How did you find us?"

"A friend of mine told me. Chris. You know him?"

All I got was a blank look; the name meant nothing.

"Young guy, twentyish, blond?"

He shook his head. "We get more and more young people coming in."

This wasn't getting me anywhere. I was going to need another meeting with Lucas. I'd have to go the old-fashioned route and push him hard. I turned and saw another face I recognized, and the synapses in my brain started fizzing.

The prostitute I'd spent a night with. I recognized her dark hair, that nose that looked like it had been broken. I watched her in profile, waiting for her to turn and notice me. I remembered our night together, when she ordered a Coke at the bar and nursed a coffee back at the flat.

Coffee, like the one she was drinking now.

Click.

I remembered that she had reminded me in so many ways of Mary, except that Mary had been drinking as if it was going out of style or as if she had a taste for it.

Click.

My brain fired off in a hundred different directions, making leaps of logic. I didn't have facts to back them up, but I knew they were true all the same.

Click.

I touched her on the shoulder, and she turned to face me, recognition burning into her face then being replaced by sadness.

"Tell me about Mary," I said.

She began to cry.

TWENTY-SEVEN

I ushered her out of the meeting and to my car.

She stayed quiet at first, speaking only to give directions. Then the CD player kicked back into life with Bob Dylan and "Rainy Day Women #12 & 35," and this was enough to get her talking.

"I love this one."

"Yeah, me too. Love how free and easy he sounds in it." I peered sideways at her. "Did I get your real name the other night?"

She smiled and seemed to think for a moment.

"Rachel."

"Nice to meet you, Rachel."

"Oh, you've already met me. That night at the flat, it wasn't my act. That was me. All the things we talked about, that was a real conversation."

Rachel offered to cook me a pasta meal as payback for the fry-up I'd done on our first night. She said the sauce was a family recipe and something I'd be amazed by. My stomach began a slow rumble at the mention of food. It had been another long day, and I just kept forgetting to eat. I stopped off on the way and ducked into an off license, not noticing my error until I was back at the car.

"Oh god, I'm sorry," I said as she opened the door for me. "I wasn't thinking."

She looked down at the wine in my hand.

"Don't worry," she said. "I'm all grown up. I can be around wine."

"You don't mind?"

"Only if I have some," she said with a smile.

Her flat was a modest ground-floor council property in the heart of Heath Town. The area was like a social experiment that threw the poor, the working class, the immigrants, and drugs into a hole to see what would happen if they were ignored. Urban redevelopment schemes kept trying to find a foothold, but knocking down the high-rise flats had just spread the problem out further. The Mann brothers owned the territory product-wise, but the streets were owned by a gang known as the Demolition Crew.

Rachel's flat was sandwiched between an abandoned building with doors and windows covered in metal plates, and a twenty-four-hour shop that was closed. All I saw on the way in was the hallway and the cramped living room, which was dominated by a futon sofa bed. The walls were decorated with film posters, just like mine. While she cooked, I hid among her record collection. It was in no order that I could work out with CDs piled one atop the other next to her stereo. Current chart music and nineties pop mixed in with old-school rhythm and blues albums. I pulled out an album I really liked, *The Church with One Bell* by John Martyn. It seemed out of place with the rest. I put it on, set the volume low, and sat on the sofa.

The meal was great, and the sauce gave her reason to be proud. It had a nice tomato tang and a spice that I couldn't identify. She drank a glass of Coke very slowly. I drank the wine a lot quicker.

"Tell me about Mary," I said again.

"What happened to her?" she said.

"She's dead," I said, before adding, "sorry."

"Who killed her?"

"I think it was her boyfriend."

"I suppose I already knew she was dead. I mean, she had to be, really. You never admit it to yourself, though, do you?"

I didn't say anything.

"You're really sure?"

"Yes."

She softened now. She appeared finally to let go of something heavy that she had been carrying around.

"Was she…," I said, not finishing the question.

"A prostitute?" She didn't seem to hide from the word. "No, she wasn't. She used to be, but she'd given it up a few months ago."

I remembered what Mary had said that night about trying to live the life she wanted, about looking for a chance.

"What was her real name?"

"Mary. She gave you her real name. She must have trusted you."

That made me feel a whole lot worse.

Mary and Rachel had met in a strip club, the "classy one out by the Desi Junction" in West Bromwich. I pretended not to know the place. Mary had come over from Ireland to work as a nurse and had started dancing to help cover the rent.

"Were you already working this night shift by then?"

"I was. I've been a prostitute pretty much my whole adult life, on and off, but Mary hadn't started it yet. She was fascinated by what I did."

"And the manager at the club didn't mind?"

"Oh, he did. He won't have hookers in his club. As soon as he found out, I was asked to leave."

"Asked?"

"Yes, he was nice enough about it. Let me work a night for free as a going-away gift, waived the stage rental."

"So when did Mary start working your job as well?"

"After she left the club. She followed me to work at Legs. The illegal place in town?"

Legs. Another Gaines connection.

"She saw me making good money on my own terms and enjoying myself every night."

"Every night?"

"Of course. I'm not going to fuck a guy I don't like the look of."

"OK."

"I gave her one of my regulars for a night, someone I trusted to be nice and friendly, and she really enjoyed it. She seemed to get off on the power of it, having a guy pay to spend time with her. That was part of the thrill of dancing, of course, but this takes it further. It was a rush for her."

"Is that what you get out of it?"

"No, I get money out of it. I think I felt the rush at first. I don't really remember."

"Did she stick with your regular guys?"

"No, she got out on her own very quick. We're very different, and guys saw different things in us."

"OK, so bring it forward a bit. You're both set up full time, and things are working, but then she stopped?"

"Yes."

"Did it affect you or upset you that this life wasn't good enough for her?"

"No, if I got upset every time a friend of mine told me they hated what I did, I'd never stop crying. And it was the right move for her. She was following me into AA, and for Mary the real battle was drugs. In this game? That's a tough fight."

"But you stayed in the business."

"I'd been at it longer, so I knew how to avoid those situations. But when someone in my line is fresh to recovery? I'd say getting out of the business is the best choice. Then she met Tommy."

The same name Bauser had given me. The same Polish guy I'd been looking for.

"Tommy?"

"Yes. He moved in quick. She said he had this smile that drove her crazy. And she loved his accent."

"Polish?"

"That sounds about right. I mean, I never asked him the details, but the accent could have been Polish, and he had that look, a bit like you."

I got taken for Polish sometimes; that came with my darker skin. White folk might not know what a Gypsy really is, but they do a great job of reminding us what we're not. Every once in a while, I thought about trying to educate people. Tell them about our Indian roots and the slow migration north. Slavery. Genocide. But I'd learned not to bother.

I'd noticed she frowned a little at the mention of his name, and I pushed. "You didn't like him?"

"No, I didn't. He was volatile. He'd lose his temper and shout at her, make empty threats. I guess after a while in my job you get a sense of guys, you can read them, and I didn't trust Tommy. He asked too many questions about the way the town worked."

"But Mary couldn't read him?"

"I think maybe she hadn't worked the job long enough or she really loved him. Who knows."

"So did Tommy make you and Mary drift apart?"

"We stopped talking for a while, yes. We never fell out. We just stopped being company for each other. Until afterward."

"Afterward?"

"She came to me a few weeks ago, really upset. Said she was in a tough spot."

"What was wrong?"

"Well, Tommy was into something. He'd been trying to set something up in town, drugs or something, and he'd pissed off the wrong people. Mary was getting dragged into it all, because she knew all the same people from her time working."

"OK, what did you say to her?"

"Get shot of it all. Go on a holiday or something. Let it all blow over."

"But she wasn't going to do that."

"No. I knew when she left here that night that she wasn't going to do what I'd said."

I told her what I knew about the business Tommy had gotten mixed up in. I held back on mentioning the needle marks I'd seen on Mary's arm. Whatever memory Rachel had of her friend, I decided to let it be the best one.

"When was the last time you saw her?" I said.

"Last weekend. She turned up here in tears. She told me she'd stolen something from Tommy and he was going to kill her."

"So what did you do?"

"Well, at first I shouted at her, shouted at her for coming here, for putting me in the way of whoever was looking for her."

"She had whatever it was they were after with her? Did you see it?"

"Oh, yes, it was a book."

"A book?"

"Yes, a black book, like an address book or a notebook."

A notebook. So that's what they had torn my house apart looking for, something that could have been hidden in my mattress or in the toilet cistern. That made sense.

"And after you'd shouted at her?"

"I tried to help. She wouldn't go to the police. I tried to tell her, but she wouldn't go, said she was in too deep."

I knew the feeling.

"So then I suggested the next best thing."

"Which was?"

She looked directly at me.

"You," she said.

The floor tilted, and I felt like I was about to fall off the edge of the world.

"What?"

"Well, after I finished shouting at her, when I climbed down off my bloody high horse, I knew we needed to find her help. I thought maybe she could still leave town. She'd always been talking about visiting her family in Ireland. I said that would be perfect."

"But she wouldn't go?"

"No. I think she had problems back home, too. So then I said we needed to find help, someone around here to look after her."

"Why me? Didn't you get the memo?"

"I saw you around when you were a cop. You always treated us with respect. We talk about things like that, you know?"

I shook my head. I didn't buy that. "A few nice smiles and cups of coffee when we're rousting you doesn't make me a nice guy."

"No, it doesn't. But a friend of mine said we should find you, that you were in with the Mann brothers, that maybe you could talk to everyone and sort it out. Said you had a bit of a hero complex."

"Who?" I already knew the answer, but I asked anyway.

"Jellyfish."

Motherfucker. I needed a new reputation, one that didn't get me mixed up in shit like this.

"Even so," I said, "what made you think I wouldn't just turn you over? If you've heard about me, then you've heard more reasons not to trust me than to think I'm any kind of hero."

"I've heard about them, yes. But you seem different, and it's not as if we had many options. It was you or Robson, and he's nasty."

"Robson?"

That was the second time I'd been given that name.

"Yeah, he also works for Gav Mann, but he's mean, always threatening people with knives. But you, I don't know, I just trusted you. You were like—" She stopped and bit back on the words, but a nod from me made her carry on. "Like a wounded little puppy. Show you some love and you'll do anything, you know?"

I didn't know whether to be offended or complimented, so I just ignored it. "What was I supposed to do? Was your plan that I would get whoever was after Mary to leave her alone? Was I meant to defend her against all comers?"

"I don't know. I wasn't thinking that far. I just wanted her to get to you and—" She stopped.

"And what?" I said.

Tears formed in her eyes again, pooling on either side of her nose and running down. "I wanted her away from me," she said in a strangled voice. "She was my friend, and all I wanted to do was get her away from me."

She rested her head on my shoulder and sobbed.

I almost felt like crying myself. A woman I had never met had decided to trust me with her life, and she was dead. And I'd dumped the body to prevent anyone from finding out. Rachel's hair fell across her face and I reached my arm round to brush it away, but that just reminded me more of Mary.

"The night you spent with me, what was that about? Did you plan that too?"

"I wanted to know what had happened. I didn't know anything. I didn't even know if Mary had found you. All I knew was that she left here in the rain and never came back."

"You could have asked me. In fact, it would have saved a lot of time."

"This week seems full of things I 'should' have done, things I didn't do, like going to the police."

"We can't do that now."

"Why not? I can just go and tell them everything I know. And you said you know for a fact that she's been murdered. You can tell them."

"No, I can't."

"Why not?" Her anger flashed then, a temper I didn't want to see put to use on my freedom or health.

"Because I'll go down with them," I said.

She looked at me blankly. Her chest jumped as if she had hiccups, and she opened her mouth to form a question. I spoke before she could put it into words.

"When I said I know she's dead, it's because I saw her. She did make it to me that night. She came back to my house, and in the morning she was dead."

I drew a breath and carried on. It felt good to be saying this out loud.

"I ran away. It's what I've always done. Run from the scene or have a good reason to be there. Run from the crime or be a cop. Then I disposed of her body to save my own skin."

There was a pause, the air in the room seeming heavy, like a gathering thunderstorm. Then Rachel slapped me, hard, across the face. The sting of the slap stayed imprinted on my face when she took her hand away, and I had to blink away a tear.

"What the hell is wrong with you?" she said.

Good question.

TWENTY-EIGHT

We sat in silence for a long time.

There didn't seem any way to restart the conversation, and the ground never opens up to swallow you when you want it to. After a while I caught Rachel staring at the wine.

"You thinking of having some?" I asked.

"No. Well, yes. But I've been sober too long to mess all that up with a stupid drink. I just find it attractive. To look at, I mean."

I understood. I can spend hours looking into whiskey or red wine or even a pint of stout as it settles.

"How long has it been? Sober, I mean."

"Five years."

"Does it get easier with time?"

"It's all very simple. You just don't drink. It's never easy, but I hate it when people make it out to be hard."

"Like people who fall off the wagon, you mean?"

"The people I know would rather chew off their hands than fall back into the bottle when problems start. But the characters on TV always start drinking again. The short-hand for a recovering alcoholic is failure."

I was glad I'd held back on telling her about Mary's drug relapse. I assumed she knew that Mary had been drinking with me, but I left that unsaid too. The silence settled between us again as the music played. John Martyn was singing "Glory Box." The anger that had flushed her face when she slapped me seemed to have gone now, and she was looking sheepish.

"Sorry, by the way," she said, giving the look a voice. "I hate it when I see *that* on TV too."

"I deserved it."

"Why did you leave the force?" Rachel looked straight at me, over the top of her glass of Coke.

I opened my mouth, beginning to go into one of my standard speeches, one of the many variations I'd used in the last few years: Paperwork. Lifestyle. Tiredness. Family. I raised the wine to my lips and drank while John Martyn sang. For some reason, I just didn't have the heart to give Rachel one of my bullshit stories.

"I didn't leave the force," I said. "I left everything. Everything I cared about. I just didn't need any of it anymore. A friend was saying the other day that I've drifted out to the edge, and I guess he's right. You know that phrase, 'The straw that broke the camel's back'?"

Rachel just nodded. I thought of all the confessions she must have heard in five years of AA meetings.

"I joined the force to fuck with my dad. I mean, why else would a Gypsy become a gavver, right? Sorry, that means cop. But then I went from hating my dad to hating everything, everything except Laura and music."

"Football?"

"Oh, no, I hate the Wolves all the time, but that's different, that's how it works when it's your team."

She smiled and nodded for me to continue. Again she brushed the hair away and again I felt a slight kick in my chest.

"When the riots kicked off in London, well, we knew something would happen up here, but nobody knew where

or how. When it started, we all went out, tried to stop it just
by being there, by talking to people. Later on, the brass wised
up, sent people out to actually deal with it as a riot, but not
at first. But it seemed like the more I was shouted at, the
more I saw anger and violence. I don't know, I just switched
off, like I started tuning out on a radio. That make sense?"

"Like static?"

"Yeah, like background noise would get more interesting
than whatever was going on, and the angrier the kids on the
street got, the more I tuned out. Then I was off duty, and it
was raining, really heavy August rain. I was driving home."
I emptied the dregs of the bottle into my wineglass. "There
was this old man in the road. He was just walking around, in
the rain. He had pajamas on and a robe, but he didn't have
a coat or anything on his feet. I got out of the car and asked
him where he was going, and he just looked at me."

I looked into Rachel's eyes, looking for something.

"Have you ever looked into the eyes of someone who's
not there anymore?"

"You mean, not there in the head?"

"Yeah. He didn't know who he was or where he was. The
best way I can describe the look is *confused*. He mumbled a
few things, but he didn't know what he was saying, there was
something missing up there. And he was soaked to the skin."

"Maybe he lived in a house in that street?"

"No. We checked. See, I took him to the hospital, and
they dried him off and put him in clean robes, but the doctors said he had real bad pneumonia. They didn't give him
long."

"What did you do?"

"Well, we checked every house in the street. Nothing.
The hospital couldn't find records on him, and he didn't
know his own name. Imagine that. No name. We tried
everything."

"Where was his family?"

"By the end, I'd realized that whoever they were, they didn't want to be found. Nobody ever came looking for him. Maybe it was the riots, or maybe someone just couldn't cope with looking after him anymore. I mean, it must be hard, looking after that. You can't expect everyone to do it."

"I suppose not."

"And the DCI couldn't give me any time or manpower. The whole world was watching the riots build up and break loose, and it was all hands to the pump, chasing kids who wanted to steal TVs and boil-in-the bag rice."

"What happened to the old man?"

"I stayed with him as he faded, sat beside him and watched buildings burning on TV. He never remembered who he was. He died with nobody. He died with no name. Can you believe that? A week he hung on, in that damned bed, with nobody."

I realized I was crying. Rachel put her hand on my arm.

"That's awful."

"And when he went, I guess he took me with him. I just couldn't stay in the world, and listening to that static was better than actually caring about something, you know? The force got me a doctor, a shrink. I think Laura pulled some strings to keep me on his list even after I left, because he won't stop pestering me."

"You ever spoken to him?"

"Once, the same day I quit. We sat in a quiet room and he asked me a lot of quiet questions. I kept wishing he would shout over the clock, its ticking was louder to me than his voice. But I told him the same thing I told Laura. Nothing is important. Nothing we do matters."

She opened her mouth as if to protest, but I kept going.

"Don't. You know it. As an adult, you know it. We live in a world where nothing we do matters."

"So what does that mean?" she said. "What does that mean we should do?"

"Nothing. We may as well do nothing. That's what I've been trying to do."

She shook her head slightly, and I knew she wanted to argue. She wanted to come up with a better philosophy, but she couldn't find the words.

"So that's why you left your wife?"

"I left her or she left me, I don't know. It's all part of the same fog. I didn't really pay attention."

I thought again of the photographs on my mum's wall. Of how I hadn't felt connected to any of them. Another time, another person, another me.

"You're wrong," she said. "You're wrong about all of that. I've gone too long sober to think there's no point to it all."

"What else makes sense? Give me a better answer."

"I'll think of one. You keep doing whatever it is you need to, and I'll think of something."

I smiled weakly. "Deal."

After a few more minutes she said she was tired. She fetched me a blanket and folded out the futon. She kissed me on the forehead, like a mother kissing her son, and then she went to bed.

I lay down on the futon, staring at the ceiling, and didn't sleep. There was no sound but the occasional noise of an early-morning drunk walking past outside, and soon I heard the slow, rhythmic breathing of Rachel as she slept. After a couple of hours I dressed and quietly left.

TWENTY-NINE

I needed to finish the thing with Chris, get it off my back. Becker wouldn't give me the information I'd asked for until I cleared this case, and my conscience wasn't going to let me sleep until I'd cleared both. I tossed and turned until dawn, then fought with the bedsheets longer until I heard the world come to life outside. I shaved and showered and ate breakfast in my shiny new kitchen. Bobby had done a great job, but he'd also made the place feel like a hotel.

I called Becker's number, and he sounded distracted when he answered. He must have had something important on, because he didn't give me a hard time.

"Listen, have you heard any rumors about Perry?"

The silence on the line was loud and clear.

"Beck, what is it?"

"It's…ahhh…" He exhaled. "Fuck it. I think he's dirty."

"Go on."

"After you asked me about enemies? Well, I asked around a bit. Trying to be subtle about it, but you know, these things always get out. So I got pulled into a meeting—it was like, you know the spy movies? Some guy talks to you in a car park and tells you to forget everything you know?"

"You met a guy in a car park?"

"Well, no, it was the superintendent's office. But I mean it was that kind of feeling, right? I got told to stop asking questions about Michael Perry and Veronica Gaines. But see, the thing was, I hadn't been asking about Gaines."

"Shit."

"Yeah. Then a little later, Laura took me for a coffee and gave me the polite version. She must have caught it in the neck, so it's not doing her job chances any good."

"Shit."

"Yeah."

"That ties into something Ash Coley said—"

"You're taking advice from Ash Coley now? Fuck's sake."

"But I think he had a point. He said that Perry would need some funding to get into politics. That's where Gaines will come in. And someone on your side knows he's at it."

"Listen, I think you should drop the case."

"What? You're the one who's been pushing me to get it done."

"Yeah, but listen. If this blows up, then I'm linked to you and you're linked to the Mann brothers, and I'm fucked. Or, the other way around, I did this as a favor to Perry, and Perry is linked to Gaines, and I'm fucked."

"Beck, there's still the issue of a missing kid—"

"No, forget it. I'll do what you asked and look into that Polish guy, but I want you to drop this. For me, OK?"

"Sure."

Like hell.

So Perry had kept company with Coley until a bigger fish came along, and now he was on a political trail funded by Gaines. She'd have no motivation for hurting Chris if she was looking to get Perry into office, but both Perry and Gaines had enemies.

Enemies much bigger and scarier than me. That doubled the threat. I had two options. Follow the money and get in over my head or follow the lies and bully Paul Lucas. Being a coward, I went with the easy route. I phoned the university to ask for an appointment with Lucas, but they told me he was about to leave the campus for a meeting.

I waited by the exit to his building and followed him when he left. The great thing about people with a secret is that they are paranoid. It shows in their walks and gives them away.

I followed him to one of the big, brand-name coffee stores. He ordered something tall and weak looking and set it down at a table with a matronly looking woman. Maybe she was his wife, maybe she was a total stranger. It's hard to tell the difference sometimes. I ordered a simple coffee and sat at a table in the corner, flicking through a sport supplement that had been left there. It was from one of the national papers and didn't cover any football teams I was interested in.

When Lucas got up for the bathroom, I followed. I moved quickly to make up the ground between us.

As soon as he was through the door, I put my hands on his shoulders and forced him against the sink.

I'd have loved to have been able to try some Chinese water torture, get a slow dripping tap on the go. But taps in these places have two settings: full and off. And they only give you a brief burst of full before stopping.

So I settled for second best and shoved the back of his head into the mirror. Not hard enough to break anything, but hard enough for him to know I was serious.

He started crying. "What the hell do you want?"

I let him rub the back of his head.

"I want Chris."

Lucas sniffed a couple times, hamming it up. "I don't know where he is. And it was wrong what you did the other night."

"The meeting? Maybe I need help."

"You were there to make a cheap point, and it was wrong."

"I didn't realize it was members only at these things."

"Bollocks. Privacy is sacred there. You violated it."

"I'll do more than barge into a meeting if you don't tell me where he is."

"What?"

"Do your employers know? How about the parents of the students?"

"You wouldn't."

"Watch me."

His eyes told me he knew I was serious. Which was good, because I wasn't so sure.

"What is this, the Salem witch trials? You have any idea what AA is about? How much good we do?"

"Oh, I know, fine. I know the good people there. I also know how easy it is to stir university people into a moral panic."

"And you'll do that to make a point?"

"No. I'll do that to find Chris."

He glared at me for as long as he could manage. Then he relaxed and gave in.

"I don't know where he is." He was telling the truth. Finally. "But I know who he's with."

He told me the name. It was short and simple. A little explosion went off in my head. Like a Magic Eye puzzle slowly coming into focus at the back of my mind, everything made sense. I knew what secret Coley had been talking about and why he'd sounded so bitter.

I knew where Chris was.

I knew what he was running from.

THIRTY

Stephanie Perry looked surprised as she opened the door to me.

I'd drifted around in my car, killing time until she would be in, and at half past five in the evening, she had bags under her eyes. The tracksuit she was wearing had seen better days.

"Oh, come in." She opened the door wider for me to walk through. "Michael's not back yet."

"I know," I said. "I didn't expect he would be. Why don't you give him a call and get him to come round?"

The surprise showed on her face again. I sat down in the living room while she picked up the phone in the hallway. She had a very brief and hushed conversation, then came through to join me.

"He'll be here in a minute," she said. "Can I get you a drink?"

"A black coffee would be great."

She left me alone while she fetched the drinks. I was sitting in the living room that bore no signs of a husband's touch, and now I knew why. I needed to know why I'd been lied to.

The doorbell rang. After another hushed conversation in the hallway, Michael Perry joined me in the living room. Stephanie followed with three mugs.

"Mr. Miller." Michael held out his hand, and I shook it. "What can we do for you?"

I took a sip from the coffee, which was very hot, very strong. "I know where your son is, Mr. Perry, and he's alive and well."

Both parents looked relieved. It almost made me let them off the hook. Almost.

"But you've been lying to me, and I need to know why."

They exchanged looks.

"I don't know what you mean," Michael said.

"OK. Tell me. When did you leave your wife, Mr. Perry?"

"What—" He sat down, his composure collapsing as I continued.

"Well, I knew something was up when we met. Sat in the pub, your local pub, with your wife, and something wasn't right. It took me until today to place it."

He just sat there. He raised his eyebrows and shook his head.

"See, what got me was when you fetched another round of drinks for you and your wife. The drink you brought back had ice in it." I turned to Stephanie. "You were hoping he'd remember how you like your vodka orange. But he didn't."

She nodded.

"See, if my wife and I have a drink together, I have to ask these things. We've been separated for a while now, and I can never remember how she takes her drinks."

Perry looked surprised. "Well, I hardly think—"

"And then, later on, you put your hand on hers and she just about jumped out of her skin. That's something you can't fake, emotion like that, a shared intimacy. You either have it or you don't. You didn't. It looked fake."

"Oh please, Mr. Miller. Is this what we paid you for?" He began to stand, as if he was going to show me to the door.

"For god's sake," Stephanie said. "Michael, enough is enough. He's found Chris. Let's hear him out."

"So you haven't been a couple for a long time," I said. "Though you are still married—I checked that. How long has it been?"

Michael gave up. "I don't know," he said. "Eleven years?"

"Twelve," said Stephanie in a very quiet voice. "Twelve years last month."

"You still live nearby, don't you?"

"Just round the corner," Michael said. "I'm never far away."

"See, there's a lot about your boy you don't know. He was hiding from something. And I couldn't figure it out. Of course, for a while I thought it was because of you." I was looking at Michael again. "But it's not that simple."

I stopped talking and drank more of my coffee, seeing how long it would take for Michael to snap. It took half the cup.

"Fuck's sake, Miller, what are you getting at?"

"You lied to me. Both of you. Holding important things back. What, exactly, did you hire me for?"

Michael looked straight into my eyes. "Whatever else you may think of us, Mr. Miller, we are parents, and our boy is missing."

I could see the parent shining through in him there, and it was about time.

"If it was so important, why hide it away by hiring me? That's what threw me. I kept looking for some big conspiracy, for the corruption that you wanted to keep hidden." He met my eyes, and a look passed between us. "How are your campaign funds doing, by the way?"

He opened his mouth and formed a few practiced rebuttals that he couldn't bring himself to throw at me before settling on a shrug.

"Relax, I don't really care." I noted the look on Stephanie's face; she didn't know about Gaines. I decided to give him a small mercy and leave it alone. It wasn't the biggest lie Perry had told. "I talked to your old friend, Ash Coley. You betrayed him too, in your own way, didn't you?"

"Ash?"

"Save it. Back to your son. I was right, Mr. Perry, there was something about you that he hated. When he realized he was the same, he started to hate himself. It must have been very hard for him to deal with."

They both stared at me.

"So tell me, Mr. Perry. Why do you hide the fact that you're gay?"

THIRTY-ONE

We were in Michael's car, parked outside the place where Chris had holed up.

It was shiny and new; it still smelled of the showroom. The only signs of life were a couple of cigarette butts in the ashtray and an empty sandwich carton at my feet. I'd never seen Michael light up, and he never smelled of firsthand smoke, so I guessed the smoker must be his partner. Michael was in the driver's seat with Stephanie next to him. I sat in the back, perched forward so that my head was almost between theirs. The windows were steamed, condensation running down the inside.

I thought back to how they'd each handled my question at the house. Stephanie hadn't shown much emotion. She remained composed through it all, almost cold. She must have done all her crying on this subject a long time ago. It was Michael who'd cried, the water welling without fuss in his eyes as he talked.

"It was hard," he said. "Even in twelve years, you can't understand how much things have changed. Maybe if it was now, if I was Chris's age, maybe it would be easier."

"I think Chris would say different," I said.

"Yes, you're right. But you can't know, Mr. Miller, how hard it is to live a lie, to be trying to live as something you aren't."

I knew too well. Chris and I weren't that far apart, living in denial and liking awkward silences, except that he seemed to be happy.

"I knew all along, of course. I think so. It's hard to explain or to put a moment to when you realize your sexuality isn't the same as everyone else's around you. When you're a boy—I'm sure you'll remember—when you're a little boy, you really aren't aware of your sexuality in one way or another. You know that there are men and women and that they're meant to fall in love at some point. You get to high school, and you know that you're supposed to fancy the girls, and you think maybe you do. I did. I really did fancy them. But I also thought the boys were cute as well. You don't understand any of this, do you?"

I'd looked him straight in the eyes. He'd looked desperate for approval.

"I think I can. Go on."

"I fancied the girls, hard not to, and Steph was so cute." His smile seemed to come from a lost age, and Stephanie joined him. In that moment, they looked like a real couple for the first time since I'd met them.

"She could have gone out with any of the boys, but she liked me, and I liked her, we got on so well. But after we, uh, well, you know. Afterward, as we were going out and things were getting serious, I knew something was wrong. It was like I realized I'd always known it. I wasn't brave enough to just come out, and I really liked Steph, so I carried on. We got jobs, a house. I tried."

Steph left the room. I thought perhaps to cry, but she returned with fresh coffee. I needed to start giving her more credit.

"When I walked out, Chris was old enough to know what was going on. I hated that part."

"You didn't hate leaving your wife?"

"Well, see, I'd lived with that for so long. Knowing I needed to do it. I was upset, but I'd been upset about it for a long time, so I was prepared. But nothing"—he paused and wiped tears away—"prepares you for walking away from your child. Nothing."

"But you did anyway."

"I was going insane. And I wasn't making Steph happy. The town, I don't mean to say it's a backwards town, but to leave your family for another man? That's something I doubt people will ever forgive. It would have made my life hell. It would have made Chris's life hell. It was really good of Steph to agree to keep it secret."

"I didn't do it for you," Stephanie said without emotion. "I did it for Chris."

She turned to me. "Mike's right, Mr. Miller. At school. Growing up. Chris would have been the butt of every joke going. I didn't want him going through that."

"So on paper, we've always been together," Michael said. "Always stayed married. Our families know the truth, and a few of our friends, but that's it. And I still think we were right."

"And you almost seem to believe yourself when you say all of that. The secrecy has nothing to do with your job, right? Wasn't it just a little bit easier to climb the ladder by leaving it out? I'm sure your political ambitions were never a factor in your bullshit either," I said, sarcasm dripping from my voice.

"That's not how it was—"

"No? And the affair you had with Ash Coley. He'll say he's just as trapped as you, I bet. He can't tell the truth about who he is without losing his power; he's terrified of the people he controls. Why did you throw him away? Was it because you were embarrassed to be gay or embarrassed to be with scum like him?"

The truth stung him, and I pressed on. "It certainly got to Chris, when you walked out. A child that age can't understand. I don't think a child twice that age can understand. He must have resented you. He hated you for leaving his mom, for leaving him, and you did it because you were gay, so he hated that as well. Then at some point, maybe the same way it happened for you, he realized he was gay too. The very thing he hated about you. That's a hell of a thing for a teenager to carry around."

Stephanie and Michael moved to hold hands. The emotion seemed genuine.

"Until he came to terms with who he was," I said, standing up and nodding for them to follow me.

I snapped back to focus in the car. Neither of the Perrys had noticed me zoning out. The rain had stepped up from a mist to a drizzle.

We'd had to rub off the car windows a few times as we sat there waiting.

"What are we doing here?" Stephanie asked.

"Just wait," I said.

Across the car park from us, one of the flats in the block came to life. A light came on in the hallway, framed by a pane of glass in the door. Through the glass we could see movement.

"OK," I said.

Jellyfish stepped out, put his hand out palm upward to check the rain, and flipped up the collar of his coat. His blonde girlfriend stepped out after him, in jeans and a three-quarter-length coat.

"There." I nodded.

Michael laughed. "That's not Chris."

"Oh god," Stephanie whispered.

"You remember telling me that Chris always liked to dress up, always liked to paint his face?"

Stephanie nodded and smiled. Michael just looked puzzled.

"Look at him, Mike. Just look." She pointed at the blonde. "Look past the hair and the coat, the makeup."

Michael squinted for a moment, then straightened up, and I knew the penny had dropped.

"Oh god."

"Doesn't he look happy, though," said Stephanie.

"Yes," said Michael. "He does."

I leaned back into the seat and watched as Jellyfish and Chris walked down the hill, headed for the town.

"Do you know the boy he's with?" Michael turned in his seat to look at me.

"I do, yes," I said.

"Is he good?"

"Honestly?"

Lie? Omit? Tell the truth?

"He's good enough."

They exchanged looks.

"What do you think we should do?" Michael said.

They both turned to look at me. I shook my head and reached for the door handle.

"You didn't pay me for that," I said.

I opened the door and stepped out into the rain. I banged a good-bye on the roof and walked down the hill toward town. Somewhere there was a drink with my name on it.

THIRTY-TWO

I woke up with a violent hangover.

I remembered drinking in Walsall and snatches of a bus ride and some ill-advised driving of my car. Then I'd somehow ended up back at Posada for last call. No lock in. I'd had enough of those. I didn't remember my dreams, and that was a good sign. Perhaps I'd had an easy night's sleep for the first time in a while. I felt a little lighter, having put one thing to bed.

I just had one more thing left to do.

The dead have a far greater hold on us than we admit. Sometimes I think the dead have a greater hold on us than the living.

My mobile rang, and I recognized the number.

"Eoin." Becker greeted me as soon as I pressed the button. "Perry called me just now. I guess you didn't do what I asked, huh?"

"Sure I did. I found the kid."

"You know what I mean. Anyway, he's happy with whatever you did, and they say they've decided to leave Chris where he is for now. Asked me to thank you and said that he won't forget that Laura or me were so supportive. Don't know what Laura had to do with anything, but never mind.

Listen, I've got some stuff for you. Can we meet up? Where are you now?"

"I'm at my house."

"I'll come round there, then?"

"No, no, it's not somewhere I like to be at the moment. How about West Park? It's just across the road from me."

"OK. On the bridge like in the spy films?"

What was it with him and spy films?

"Sounds good. Fifteen minutes?"

"Twenty."

Fifteen minutes later I was leaning on the side of the bridge, watching the ducks when Becker approached from the far side of the park.

"Just like in the spy films," I said.

"I suppose we should have brought bread for the ducks," Becker said.

"So what have you got for me?"

"I really don't know, exactly, but I think you can tell me. But Eoin, whatever it is, it's trouble."

"What makes you say that?"

"You said you wanted to know about a Polish drug dealer, name of Thomas?"

"Yes."

"Well, that sort of matched with something I'd seen. It jogged something, and I needed to look into it before I could give you anything."

He pointed off to our left, and we walked to a bench.

"I remembered, a while ago, hearing about this case. But it wasn't me who picked it up."

He stopped talking while a young couple walked past, really playing up the man-of-mystery role. He had me hooked.

"A few weeks back, this guy was pulled in for questioning." Becker reached inside his jacket and pulled out a photocopied sheet of paper that he passed to me. "He was arrested in the Apna pub for possession with intent. The arresting uniform found class-A narcotics on his person and reported finding a lot more in the suspect's car."

"How much?"

"Difficult to say."

"Why? It would be in the report."

"I'll get to that in a minute."

I looked at the paper he'd handed me. It was a copy of a passport identifying one Thomasz Janas, a Polish national who had entered the United Kingdom eight months previous. Now I had a face to put to the name. He looked cold and mean but youthful, like a young man who was learning the trade the hard way.

"I know why he was arrested because I remember talking to the uniform in the canteen around that time. 'Course, this was back when we still had a canteen. Did I tell you they closed them down to make way for prayer rooms?"

"Beck—"

"Yeah, OK, anyway. He was bragging to me about his case, kidding himself into thinking he'd get any of the credit. Anyway, he told me there was enough heroin and cocaine in the guy's car to buy a brand-new Mercedes."

"Simple case, then?"

"It would seem. But then the guy, this Janas, he was released after two days in custody. All charges dropped."

"Have you guys made it legal now to carry coke and H?"

"No way, not this side of an election," he deadpanned. "It's strange. The official report shows no mention of either. It states that after the arrest, he was searched and found to be in possession of an eighth of marijuana. He was told off for smoking, warned of the health and legal risks, and sent on his way. I checked the intranet and the EFB. There's no record of anything else."

"So the uniform lied about the arrest?"

Becker stared at the lake for a while. "I don't believe he did, no. I tracked him down yesterday and asked him about it again. Subtle, like. He has no idea that Janas walked. He told me he'd been asked to keep the case quiet. Promised a part in court once the trial went ahead."

"What's his name?"

"Joe Murray. I don't think you'll know him."

"No, name doesn't ring any bells."

"Trust me, this guy's no bright spark. By the time he wakes up enough to start asking questions, he'll have lost out on any leverage he ever had. He's never getting out of that uniform. What do you know about Janas?"

"He's a dealer, a big one. He's been getting drugs into town and selling them cheap. Taking business from both Gaines and the Mann brothers."

Becker shook his head. "Jesus," he said.

"Exactly."

"How do you see it?"

"Someone at your place set this guy loose and managed to lose the evidence. That means one of two things."

He nodded. "Either he's been set up as a grass or it's, well…" He rubbed the bridge of his nose. "Another fucking cover-up."

Becker shuffled in his seat. "There is a third option, you know. It could be that someone is building this as a big case. Something to build a career on, you know?"

And right there, I knew why he was uncomfortable. I knew why he was trying to convince me of a third option even before we'd discussed the first two. I turned and looked straight at him.

"Laura," I said.

He nodded.

"She was the case officer. It's her report that writes him off as a pot smoker. The real story did a runner between the arrest and her report."

"Have you listened to the interview tape?"

"Yes. It matches everything in the written report. Janas is questioned about his usage and given a telling off. The usual script."

"So somewhere between Murray making an arrest for possession and Laura pressing record on the interview tape, Janas managed to lose a stash of class-A drugs and become an idiot stoner."

Fuck.

My wife was in this. She'd covered up Janas's trail and let him go. What was she getting herself into?

"Look, you and I both know that she wants that DCI office permanently and that she's not got enough pull to get it yet. But if she managed to bring together a major drug bust under everyone's noses, she'd be set for her entire career."

"You think she's just sandbagging?" I asked.

"Playing it slow, yes. Maybe sitting on the real report so that nobody steals the case or turning this guy loose to grass for her. Either way, she's sitting on a hell of a case here."

I could practically hear the cogs spinning in his head.

"No," I said.

"What?"

"You're not going to find a way to muscle in and share it. You're not going to mention it to her. And you're not getting any more involved than you already are."

"So what do I get out of all this?"

"You got a beaten pensioner and a gay student. You should be happy."

"Gay?"

"Long story."

I stood up and left him alone with his questions. I had too many questions of my own bubbling around in my head and not enough answers to go around. I had a sinking feeling that I couldn't shake—the feeling that I was in way over my head.

THIRTY-THREE

Traffic was going from bad to worse.

The Wolves were playing at home in a few hours, it was an important game and the roads were getting crowded. I almost felt the match-day buzz. It would have been the first time in a long time.

Laura had moved into a brand-new two-bedroom apartment on the corner of Key Gardens and Jeremiah Road. The estate had been called Saint Peter's Walk back when we first looked at it. It was part of the very same urban renewal program that was driving the problems to new ground in Heath Town. A collection of three- and four-story houses along with apartment buildings, Saint Peter's Walk wanted to feel like a gated community but without the gates. With the snarling traffic, it took me twenty minutes to do a half-lap of the ring road and find her apartment complex. As I drove I tried to think of tactful ways of addressing the subject of Thomasz Janas. I couldn't think of a single way that didn't either implicate me in murder or accuse her of covering up a crime. I decided to give up planning ahead and just wing it. Why change the habit of a lifetime?

I parked around the corner from the apartment building and walked round.

I'd never been inside, but from the outside it looked like everything she was and I wasn't. Clean, modern, and well appointed. I imagined the usual pastel colors and simple white furniture. A pile of magazines on a coffee table. Maybe a photograph of us somewhere, hidden away in a shoebox. The kitchen would be the sparest room; I was always a better cook than she was. She wouldn't have a cupboard full of spices or a fridge full of food.

As I rounded the corner, I caught sight of a familiar car. It was the same car that Bull had forced me into on the way to visit the sports club, and Bull was leaned against it, smoking a cigarette. He hadn't noticed me, and I hung back out of sight.

I tried not to look at him, to turn my attention to the passing traffic, for fear of him feeling my stare. He shifted his weight on the car, and for a moment I thought he was going to turn and look my way, but he merely turned toward the car and opened the rear door nearest the curb. No sooner had he done so than the front door of one of the ground-floor apartments opened and Veronica Gaines walked out.

In the doorway I saw Laura, and the bottom dropped out of my stomach. In fact, the bottom dropped out of my world completely.

Veronica turned and said something to Laura, who extended her hand with a thin smile. Gaines took it in a quick shake before nodding a good-bye and ducking into the car.

Bull walked round to the other side and let himself into the back of the car. After a moment the car pulled away from the curb and vanished around the far corner, back into traffic. Laura looked around as if she felt me watching, then shut the front door.

I was numb.

Laura had let Janas go.

Janas was in hiding.

Veronica Gaines had warned me off the case.

Laura had warned me off the case.

They were both mixed up in it somehow, and now it seemed they were mixed up in it together. What the hell was going on?

Laura seemed surprised to see me.

She stood in the doorway for a moment without speaking before cocking her head to one side.

"I didn't expect to see you," she said.

Subtext: *How long were you out there? What did you see?*

"I thought I'd surprise you," I said.

Subtext: *I'm not sure what I've just seen, but I'm sure you know I've seen it.*

She turned and walked inside the flat, leaving the door open for me to follow. The small hallway opened onto a large living room. It was not quite as I'd imagined it. The floor was hardwood, and the furniture matched it, aside from the wooden sofa's pale-blue cushions. Besides unread magazines, the coffee table held a pile of paperwork and two coffee cups. Her work clothes were slung over the back of an armchair against the far wall awaiting ironing. Next to the television on a wooden entertainment unit was a turned-down picture frame. I wanted to see the photograph, but I'd need to distract her first. The room still smelled of Veronica Gaines's perfume, and my memory kicked me in the back of the head. It was the same perfume Laura had worn at Bauser's funeral, and I'd not made the connection.

The silence was broken as some people walked past outside singing football songs.

"You going to the game?" Laura asked as she cleared away the coffee cups.

"No. Becker is, though."

"He told me you'd found the missing student. Good work."

"Thanks. He told you the rest?"

She shrugged. It said, I already know.

"So Perry's going to be allowed to carry on?"

She shrugged again. "Why not?"

"I suppose to expose him now would smear the force. Why spill all that blood when you can have a pet commissioner?"

"Something like that."

She took the cups through to the kitchen, and I heard them clink as she set them down. Then I heard the sound of a kettle boiling and more cups being fetched out of a cupboard.

"Do you have sugar?" she called out.

"No thanks," I said. While she was in the kitchen, I looked at the turned-down photograph. It was of the two of us a couple hours after the wedding. I was in a casual shirt and dark trousers, and she was wearing a black dress. We were both grinning like children.

My heart skipped a beat at the thought that she still kept the photo on display. Then I drifted to the obvious question. Why was it facedown?

Did she not want Veronica Gaines to see it?

I put it back as I'd found it when I heard her footsteps and turned as she stepped back into the room, holding two fresh mugs of coffee. She handed one to me and then sat on the sofa. I sat next to her.

"Listen, about the other night—"

She had cracked first, but I was losing interest in keeping score.

"Don't worry about it," I said. "Bad timing, that's all."

She nodded, and we settled into silence again. Familiar. Expected.

I looked around at the expensive furnishings. If not for Gaines's perfume hanging in the air, I half expected I'd be able to smell fresh paint.

"Nice place," I said. "The rent decent?"

She shook her head. "No rent. I own it."

Interesting. She owned the flat just as I owned the house. I thought back to what she'd asked me the other night. *What happened to us?*

"So it's half mine then? Wow, I have better taste than I thought."

She laughed it off, and we eased back into the seat. I smiled at her, and she smiled back. In my head I was still trying to find a way into it, the correct question to ask. I didn't want to give anything away.

"Who was the cute woman I just saw you with?"

I watched her eyes as her brain ticked away. She knew. The fact that I knew about Perry's dirty secrets told her I knew who Gaines was.

"Just a friend. She runs a local community program."

I just sat there and nodded, watching her reaction. We never could completely bullshit each other. It had been part of what had made us work and what had torn us apart. We read each other better than anyone else.

"Are you getting involved with her program?"

"It's not really my scene. But she has some good ideas, so I'm helping her out a little. You know, it helps the career."

"Sounds interesting."

"It's really not. I'm already thinking it might be a waste of time. Thinking I might pull out before it becomes too much of a commitment, you know?"

"Just make sure you don't get dragged in over your head. You could get dragged into something against your will, like me."

"I don't believe that," she said.

"Don't believe what?"

"The part about it being against your will. I've known you a long time now, Eoin, and you never do anything you don't want to."

I made a noise of protest, and she put up her hand.

"You quit a job that everybody told you to stay with. You left a marriage that everybody wanted you to work on. You've worked for people that all of your friends have told you to avoid. And now you've clearly found something else to worry about. None of that was ever against your will." Laura was peering at me intently, as though reading something written at the back of my eyes. "Why are you here, Eoin?"

"Trying to see if you need my help, I suppose."

"There you go. Trying to be a knight in shining armor."

"A knight in rusty armor, maybe."

"Old gold," she said.

"What?"

"Wolves' color, right? A knight in old gold armor."

I laughed and pretended not to like that. How had she turned this into a conversation about me? Part of my brain was telling me she'd scored again.

"You're never as hard or cynical as you'd like people to think." Laura set her drink down on the coffee table and then put her hands on mine. "Don't worry about me," she said. "I know what I'm doing."

That was as close to it as she was going to let me get.

"I hope so," I said.

Because I sure as hell didn't.

THIRTY-FOUR

I needed to think, so I stopped at the supermarket for supplies before driving back home to cook and listen to music.

I put a couple of baguettes in the oven to warm and
started a fresh pot of coffee brewing. As John Prine sang
"Souvenirs" through my stereo speakers, I chopped and
diced. I set some vegetables sizzling in a pan, pulled a
pack of pork out of the fridge, and decided which spices
to throw in.

The lyrics to the song bounced around my head. They
seemed to fit Laura and me perfectly.

I needed to find the notebook, that was still clear. It was
what Mary had stolen, and it was what Janas had destroyed
my house looking for. If I found it, I could bring him out
of hiding. But then what? Laura was involved with Gaines
somehow and knew Janas. I couldn't go to the police. I'd
managed to get myself in too deep for that. Was it too late
to go to the Mann brothers? Another fine mess I'd gotten
myself into.

The notebook wasn't in my house. It couldn't be. Janas
had known what he was looking for and hadn't found it. My
brain fizzed as I made another connection that should have
been obvious. Posada had been broken into, but nothing
much had been taken. That was where Mary had met me,

and that was another place the notebook could have been stashed. Had Janas found it?

I turned the meat over in the pan and piled the cooking vegetables on and around it, turning it around with my wooden spoon, hearing the sizzle almost drown out the music. I threw a pinch of turmeric and cayenne pepper into the pan and mixed it all together. It smelled good, and my world full of worries dropped away for a moment, then drifted back into my mind in some sense of order.

Draw Janas out into the open, hand him over to either Gaines or the Mann brothers, then walk away and forget it all.

On the stereo, John Prine gave way to Sugar. Bob Mould was singing about standing on top of the Hoover Dam and making a deal with the devil.

As I turned the heat off below the pan, my mobile rang. Everyone had the number, it seemed, except me.

"Eoin?" Rachel sounded a bit shaken on the other end.

"What's up?"

"My flat's been broken into."

"Hang on a sec." I pinned the phone between my ear and the crook of my shoulder so that I could continue dishing up the food. "What did you say?"

"My flat. It's been trashed."

"Does Mary's boyfriend know where you live?"

The uncertain silence on the other end was enough of an answer. I set the pan down on the counter and concentrated on the phone.

"Rachel, pack a bag and come round to my place. Now."

I gave her my address and ended the call. I cut the two baguettes open and split the contents of the pan between them. By the time I'd got the food set out onto two plates and two mugs of coffee poured out, Rachel was at the front door.

"You get a taxi?"

She nodded. She looked shaken, which would have been natural enough after a break-in, but this was worse. She'd put two and two together and gotten the same answer as me.

"He was after the notebook," she said. "He must think I have it."

"Do you?"

She gave me a look that told me to stop being stupid.

"Stay here for now," I said. "He's already trashed this place, so he won't come back unless we give him reason to. I'll figure out the rest later."

"You want to find the book before he does?"

"Yes."

"And when you've found it, he'll come for you. What then?"

"You don't want to know."

We sat in silence while we ate. The food tasted great, the coffee tasted awful. You can't win them all. Halfway through the baguette, she looked up at me with a smile, as if she'd just remembered a joke.

"I've been doing some reading," said Rachel.

"What kind of reading?"

"For my project, my 'you' project."

I laughed in spite of myself.

"There was a guy called Warren Zevon who died a few years ago."

"Yes, I know. He sang "Werewolves of London." Recorded an album as he was dying. I think I've got a copy."

"OK. But do you know what he said before he died?"

"He said, 'Enjoy every sandwich.'"

"Oh, OK, so you've already heard it."

"Rachel, was this meant to be the great new philosophy for me to adopt?"

"Well, it was just an idea."

"The motto that was going to get my life back on track?"

"I can see it was maybe flawed."

"To enjoy every sandwich?"

"Well, sandwiches are nice."

"Oh, I know. I already enjoy every sandwich, but my skills at eating two slices of bread hasn't stopped me from—" I stopped dead. I was far more comfortable with admitting I had a problem than I was with finding a name for it. "You know, the whole 'not caring' thing."

"OK, so quoting dead musicians probably isn't going to help you."

"No, it really won't. Although it won't make things any worse. Unless you start quoting Kurt Cobain."

"OK, I guess I'll go back to square one."

Boom.

"What did you say?"

"I'll start again, go back to square one. You know, think it all through from the beginning."

A huge grin must have hit me, because then Rachel smiled as well. The beginning. There was one place Janas wouldn't know to look, and I should have known it straightaway.

I leaned over and kissed Rachel on the cheek.

"You are brilliant," I said.

"Pretty much, yes. But why?"

"Tell you later." I grabbed my car keys and jacket and stood to leave. "Make yourself at home."

I left and headed for Posada.

Where it had all started.

I pushed through the front door, barely responding to the greetings. Now I knew where the book had to be. Anybody following Mary would have known to search the bar area, just as anybody following us would have known to search my house. But there was a place they didn't know to search, a place the two of us had sat that night after the pub closed.

I walked through to the back, to the corner table where we had sat. Most of the match goers had already started making their way down to the stadium, so Posada was quiet enough for the table to be unoccupied. Ignoring the sniggers and questions of the people at the bar, I got down on my knees. Being this close to the carpet in a pub is not a nice experience; you can smell every drunken night, every weak stomach or spilled pint. I pushed that aside and focused on what I was down there for. The seat she had sat on was a booth seat, fixed to the wall, with a space underneath where heating pipes ran along the skirting board. I reached my hand under and felt around. It took me a minute, a minute of touching old beer mats and a crisp packet that the cleaner had missed, but my hand closed around something.

The notebook.

It looked a lot like mine, but bigger. It was battered and well thumbed. I sat at the table and flipped through it.

It contained a mix of names, dates, phone numbers written in scrawling handwriting, someone who wasn't comfortable with the English version of the alphabet. I saw phone codes for Newcastle, Birmingham, Wolverhampton, Glasgow, and London. There were foreign numbers, area codes that I didn't recognize, and postal details as varied as Poland, Ireland, and Afghanistan. There were pages full of numbers, like a coded version of an accounts ledger, and names of local pushers, some with ticks next to their names and some with crosses. My name and address was on there with a question mark next to it.

In the right hands, this was a business empire; either Gaines or the brothers could use this to take over the routes. The police could use this to cripple an industry. This was like rocket fuel in my hands, waiting for someone to supply a match.

And it was going to find me a killer.

THIRTY-FIVE

The question now was how long it would take.

Janas surely had someone keeping an eye on me, and word that I'd found the book would reach him soon enough. I needed to speed things up, though. It was time to start pissing people off again, to start setting the pace instead of chasing the game.

I held the book in my hand for all to see as I left the pub. I crossed over to the churchyard and found Matt wrapped in a tattered Wolves scarf to complement his army jacket.

"I've found it," I said.

"Found what?"

"It. Just spread the word. Tell everyone you see."

I left him to it and started talking to the same street dealers I'd spoken to when this all started. I dropped Janas's name to them and made sure they saw I was carrying a notebook. I called in to the local radio station to speak on its football phone-in. The presenter welcomed me on air and asked me to predict today's score. I said one-nil and then announced that I'd found the notebook. He was asking me what I meant by that as I hung up.

I walked round to the post office and bought a pack of A4 paper, a marker pen, and cello tape. Then I drove back to my house. With Rachel watching, I stuck together enough sheets of paper to make a banner. Using the marker pen I wrote a message.

I'VE GOT THE BOOK.

Big and bold.

I taped the banner to my front window from the inside, then locked up and left after telling Rachel to stay out of sight upstairs for a few hours.

That should be enough. Now I could settle into Posada with a comfortable pint and wait for Janas to come and find me. The football game had just kicked off, so traffic was light. It would have taken a couple of minutes to drive into the city center and find a parking space, but I decided to walk instead. As I passed Molineux, I could hear the songs and the chants of the crowd at the game. After a minute, I heard a loud cheer, followed by goal music over the tannoy. My heart skipped for the first time in a long time at the thought of the Wolves scoring. It felt important again.

I was waiting at the traffic lights on the ring road as a familiar figure hobbled toward me. It was Lee Owen, his arm in a cast and his left knee buckling as he walked. As he drew near I saw the swelling around his right eye and stitches along his hairline. The fingers of his broken arm stuck out from the end of the cast, but I only counted three.

We stared at each other as he passed me.

"Fucking cunt," he said over his shoulder as he shuffled along the road in the direction I'd just come.

I'd earned that, I supposed, so I let it go.

I crossed the road when the lights changed, and it wasn't until I reached the other side that I realized what I'd just seen and why it mattered.

I still had the keys to the low-rise flat on Junction Road. I let myself in to the building and climbed the stairs to the level I'd been staying on a few nights before. The first door

I came to was where I'd met Bobby when he'd given me the
keys, where I'd interrupted him as he worked.

I put my ear to the door and listened. No sounds came
from inside. I stepped back from the door and looked
around me. I leaned over the balcony to look down at the
car park. Nobody was around.

I fumbled with my keys until I found the one for the flat
I'd been using and tried it in the lock. It slid in but wouldn't
turn. No good. Time for another trick of the trade. Another
key on my key ring was a filed-down Yale; all of the tips had
been smoothed over with a penknife's metal file until they
were of the same low height. I pushed the key three-quarters
of the way into the lock. After taking another look around,
I took off my shoe and used it as a hammer, hitting the end
of the key so that it surged into the lock with force. The door
clicked open.

They actually taught me that on the force. Preparing me
for a life of crime, one way or another.

I replaced my shoe and pushed the door the rest of the
way open. In the hallway, I was hit by the smell and a now-
familiar feeling. Now I knew how a building felt when it had
a dead body in it.

The living room and kitchenette were decorated the same
as the flat I'd used. The bedroom had been used recently—
the bed was rumpled, and the smell of sweat and deodorant
was in the air—but there was nothing in it of interest to me.
It was in the bathroom that I found the corpse.

Dumped in the bath, a thick layer of congealed blood in
the bottom, was the broken body of a man. Blades and tools
were arrayed on the floor, and in the corner was a bucket
filled with lime and a roll of bin liners. Somebody would be
coming back to clear away the remains.

I didn't think the man had been dead for very long. His
skin still felt human to the touch, not hard and rigid like

Mary's when I'd found her in the boot. I didn't touch him more than once, though, for fear of leaving evidence. Had I not known better, I would have believed he had been mauled by a bear. The fingers were missing from his right hand. His left hand was tucked out of sight beneath him. His right leg twisted in unnatural ways, and his teeth were lying in the blood in the bottom of the bath. His face was puckered and swollen, and his jaw didn't line up correctly with the rest of his head. He'd been tortured more than my stomach could handle, and I backed out of the room and crouched in the hallway until I could breathe again.

When I'd met Bobby here, he'd said he was feeding someone with a broken jaw. I'd heard the whimpers myself and made the assumption it was Lee Owen in there. Because in my head the whole world revolves around me. But I'd just seen Owen, and his jaw wasn't broken.

The name I'd heard twice in the last few days, Mr. Robson, fizzed in my mind. In a town obsessed with football, there would be an obvious nickname for someone with that surname.

Bobby.

Bobby fucking Robson.

Every football fan in England would make that connection it seemed, except for me. But then, I'd never supported the English national team. I pretended that gave me an excuse for missing the obvious. I spent about ten seconds wondering what his real first name was, but some mysteries don't matter even to me. It was his surname that had done me. It was all so silly that I couldn't help but sit and giggle for a while. Bobby was involved. Slow Bobby. Fast Bobby. Quiet Bobby. Quiet enough to have sneaked into my house and killed Mary without waking me, quiet enough to have stood behind me taking pictures. He'd been at my house when it was trashed, and he could have used decorating it as an excuse to take a further look. The reason I'd always found him so useful was that people underestimated him, but it had been me doing that all along.

I felt the buzzing at the base of my skull. The world felt distant again and the world's background noise started to sweep in over me. I fought it back. Not now.

Bobby was the killer.

And the man in the bathtub, even broken and swollen, was recognizable from his passport picture as Thomasz Janas.

THIRTY-SIX

I counted to ten.

Then I counted to ten again, but all the counting in the world wasn't going to make things better, no matter what the marriage counselors might say.

I crouched in the hallway, breathing through my mouth and trying not to smell the corpse. Bobby would have to come back soon to deal with it. He could have dealt with Mary too, but he'd dropped her in my lap. I'd thought I'd just about gotten a handle on things earlier this day. I'd been bracing myself to find out that my wife was involved and that the Mann brothers could bail me out.

Now it seemed, one way or another, everyone I knew was involved. And the sick joke of it was the question I'd asked Gav outside The Robin the night this had all started: "Business close by?" Sure enough. He'd been here when I'd called him. If I had to make a guess at what he'd been up to, torturing Janas was probably a good bet. The Robin was only a couple minutes away, which was why he'd turned up so fast.

The walls closed in around me for a second.

My father's voice was in my head again, telling me to run. Telling me this was a situation I couldn't win. Well, the voice was right. I was in way over my head. But I never do the right thing at the right time. Running had gotten me nothing so far, and I had to do something to get Mary out of my dreams.

I checked that I'd not left any traces of my visit and let myself out of the flat, making sure the door locked firmly as I pulled it shut. I called Gav Mann, and the phone didn't ring for long.

"I think we need to talk," I said when he answered.

"Do we?"

"Nobody been talking to you today? You not listened to the radio?"

He paused long enough for me to know he knew exactly what I was talking about.

"You have something of mine," he said at last.

"Yes, I do."

"OK. Where do you want to talk?"

"Somewhere public. West Park, by the bandstand. And Gav? Come alone."

"How do I know you'll be on your own?"

"Who the hell do I have?"

He laughed.

He was just bigheaded enough to underestimate me, the same way I'd always underestimated Bobby. I told him to meet me there in half an hour and disconnected the call. I made two more calls before heading home.

The house was silent, which meant Rachel was doing as she'd been told. I called out for her to come downstairs, and after a moment I heard her soft footsteps on the landing and she appeared at the top of the stairs. She looked sleepy and scared.

I smiled at her, but I must have been looking even worse than she was, because it only seemed to make her more worried.

"What's happening?"

"Don't worry about it. Get your coat and bag. I've got a friend coming to pick you up."

"What's wrong with staying here? You'd said Tommy wouldn't—"

"Tommy's dead. Like I said, get your coat."

I told her as much of it as I'd pieced together, leaving out the details about the amount of pain Janas must have gone through in his last days.

The front doorbell rang, followed by a couple of swift knocks on the door. I opened the door to find Jellyfish grinning at me from behind a pair of fake Ray-Bans, giving it the full Jack Nicholson.

"Thanks for coming." I turned to let him in. Jelly waggled his eyebrows instead of shaking hands. I poked him in the ribs. "Is your fella in the car?"

Jelly pointed out to where his car was parked across the end of my driveway. He waved at Chris, who was sitting in the front passenger seat. Chris didn't wave back; he seemed to be messing with the radio.

"How did you know about him?"

"His parents hired me to find him."

"No shit?"

"I told them you were a good boy, so this is where I need you to prove me right. You're part of this, and I need you to keep Rachel safe for a while."

Jelly made a show of a lewd grin, bowed, and picked up Rachel's bag. She turned and gave me a small kiss on the cheek. "Be careful."

As she walked toward the car, I leaned in close to Jelly.

"That goes for you too. Behave."

He grinned and skipped to the car. As they pulled away, I locked up the house and left.

West Park is a nice place to visit if you like greenery and open spaces. It's even better if you like a boating lake and some pointless statues. In the distance I could still hear the sound of the crowd at the football game. The stadium was just a couple of streets away, and the crowds would be pouring out in another twenty minutes. For now the park was almost deserted. A few families were braving the cold on the boating lake, and a couple of teenagers lay stoned on the grass.

I climbed the steps to the bandstand and leaned on the railing.

As far as plans went, I had one. It was a flawed plan, though, because it had a more than 50 percent chance of getting me killed.

THIRTY-SEVEN

Gav Mann was ten minutes late in meeting me.

He swaggered up to the bandstand with a bottle of Maker's Mark bourbon in his hand. He passed it to me with a wide-beam grin.

"Peace offering, man."

I took the bottle and turned it over a couple of times, inspecting the work of art, the dripped wax effect and the old brown label. He offered his right hand for a shake. I shook my head instead and leaned back on the railing, setting the bottle beside me.

"So you've got a present for me in return?"

I didn't answer. I just stared off toward the lake.

"Come on, man, don't play it like this. We're still buddies, yeah?"

I turned and looked him up and down as coolly as I could manage. "Were you in my house that night or was it just Bobby?"

If he was surprised, he didn't show it.

"That's what we like about you, Eoin. One way or another, you get the information."

"Why didn't you come to me from the beginning?"

"You mean in the house?"

"No. I mean the beginning. You wanted to find the Pole, you wanted to find his stash. Why didn't you come to me?"

"You have no stomach for it, Eoin. That's why we didn't come to you. You may like to play bad guy, but you're not. You've never got involved in the game."

"Why didn't you come to me about the girl?" I said. "When she came looking for me. That's what she did, you know. She came to me because she thought I could protect her from you. She thought you and I would work out a deal and everything would be OK."

He smiled. "What would you have done? Handed her over? You don't know when to run and when to fight. We needed to know if we could trust you, which side you were on. You've still got the stink of cop on you when it comes to some things. We needed to know if you were really with us yet."

"And killing a girl in my house tells you that?"

"Killing her in your house was just convenient. It was the first chance we got. I tell you, when we thought she was running to the police station, we were fucked. But then she went running to you instead, and we knew we'd be OK."

I ignored that, or tried to. I opened the bottle of Maker's and buried the sting of his words with whiskey.

"Where does the trust come into it?"

"That's where it got fun. If you'd woken up and she'd been gone, you wouldn't have known anything. I bet you'd never have given her a second thought. Yeah, I'm right. Thing is, this was a chance to test you. I figured if you saw the body you'd have two options. Call the police and prove you're with them or call me and prove we can trust you."

"I didn't do either."

"No. That's your problem, right there. You took the third option, you always do, Gyp. Like I said before, you don't know when to stand or when to run."

"So then you figured you couldn't trust me and I had the notebook. You used the photographs to fuck with me."

He laughed as if we were remembering a childhood prank.

"Yeah, and putting the body in your car later? That was my brother's idea. He can be a devious fuck when he wants."

He pulled an envelope out of his jacket pocket and let it sit on the rail between us. I refused to look at it. I didn't want to start wondering just how much cash was inside.

"You were not born stupid, Eoin, you just act like it."

"It was my house," I said through gritted teeth.

"And I'm sorry about that and for all the damage we did. We covered that with the decorating. Don't try and tell me the house doesn't look ace. And after all, it was our money that paid the mortgage, wasn't it?"

I took a mouthful of Maker's and let it burn my throat, the heat fading down into my gut and not making me feel any better.

"So what was the order? You met Mary on the street?"

"Yeah. I used her a few times. We used her to get information on Gaines from that baps and flaps club."

Legs. Rachel had told me Mary worked there for a while.

"Then when you found out she knew the Pole, you leaned on her to get you what you needed."

"Sounds like you've got it all straight. I don't need to tell you anything."

"What happened that night?"

"She was supposed to meet us and give us the Pole's notebook, so we could do it all clean. No blood, you see? We tried. But she backed out, said she wouldn't betray him. Don't know why, the Polish fuck was always threatening her. She'd told us about it. Then they had some kind of argument, and we had to make our move. We grabbed him, but he didn't have the book. When we heard that she was talking with you in Posada, we knew we could leave her there for a while. We were walking behind you when you left, but you were both too drunk to care."

I gripped the bottle with both hands but didn't lift it off the rail.

"Robson is so good at breaking in, he can get in anywhere without a sound. We waited downstairs while you two, well, you know. What you didn't do. I have to say, Eoin, you are a heavy sleeper when you're drunk."

I was sure the glass was going to break in my hand.

"You killed her. You killed her in my bed. My house."

"She was just a nobody. In the wrong place, with the wrong guy, and nobody is going to miss her. Not even the police care."

"And Janas, you killed him too. And not quickly, from what I saw."

"We needed him to talk. We thought he could tell us what was written in the notebook, but he didn't remember it all. We let him stare at his dead girlfriend for a day or so before we put her in your car, but that didn't help him remember anything. He did give up Bauser, though."

Bauser. He was killed because Janas had named him. Nothing to do with me.

"He was a good kid."

"Yeah, he was. But he'd been cheating us. And we have a business to run. You know how it is."

"Business?"

"All it ever is, Gyp. It's all it ever is. Bauser was a business decision, just like the Pole and just like your dead girl."

"Mary." I practically growled it out. "Her name was Mary."

"Yeah, whatever."

He picked up the envelope.

"You found something for us; it's what you do. So we don't have any problem here, do we?"

He began counting fifty-pound notes out onto the rail.

What I thought was anger, cold rage building in me, turned to frustration.

I watched the money stacking up in front of me. The blood money on the wooden perch in front of me mixed with the alcohol in my system. I could take the money. I could have another drink, then another, and after a while this would all fade into nothing. Because I was right in what I'd said to Rachel. Nothing we do matters.

My father's hands pressed on my shoulders as I heard his voice again. I always feel them on my shoulder when I remember him.

"They won't ask questions. They won't stop to see who else might have done it. They will kick the shit out of you and lock you up. If your hands are out of sight, they'll assume you've got a knife. Whatever happens out there is not your concern. Walk away."

I left the whiskey in my mouth, warm on my tongue, and then swallowed it back. My eyes watered. I started counting out the money.

My father's hand squeezed my shoulder again.

"If there's trouble, be far away. If you can't be far away, run like hell."

I could take the money and run.

THIRTY-EIGHT

I stared into the bottle as my body shook and my mind burned.

Gav Mann was talking, but for a while I wasn't listening. I was far-off, thinking of cookery and music and my conscience. Thinking of dead women and dead boys and their mothers at funerals. And I was thinking about the money.

"It was my house," I said.

"Look—"

"It was my house. All I wanted was a house. Where nobody could touch me."

To be nothing like my father was what went unsaid, *to deny who I really am.*

He put his hand on my shoulder and grinned.

"Look, Eoin, I'm sorry about the way things have gone, all right? We should have come to you." He guided me toward the steps of the bandstand. "Come on, I'll take you to Angels or the Apna. Get you drunk, get you laid. Let's go."

The smile didn't leave his face.

I picked up the money and pocketed it. I gave him a smile that I hoped didn't reveal a tenth of what I was thinking.

"The book's over the road at my house. Come on."

I walked on ahead, and I could feel the beam given off by his smug grin as he followed. He would have been feeling pretty good with himself at that point, and it was a feeling that would have lasted until we were crossing the footbridge over the boating lake.

When we were halfway across, Veronica Gaines and Bull stepped onto the bridge ahead of us. Bull was carrying a cricket bat, and Gaines was carrying a nasty smile.

"What the fu—"

Gav turned, but more men were blocking the way we had just come. They looked like they'd been eating steroids their whole lives. And they seemed to like cricket.

I spun on the balls of my feet to get right into Gav's face.

"Her name was Mary. *Mary*. And Bauser's name was *Eric*. I bet you didn't even know that, did you?"

"You're fucking dead," he said.

He lunged toward me, his fist connecting with my stomach. I stepped back and caught my breath.

"You've ruined everything," he said. "Over a woman, a stupid fucking woman."

The coldness in me took over, but it didn't make me sink away from the world; this time it made me more alive. I hit him. I hit him again. The old man in the street. Laura. Mary. My job. Every emotion and every conversation I'd not been able to process suddenly wanted to jump out of me, into my fist, and do some serious damage. I swung the bottle of whiskey at him with my other hand. He fell against the side of the bridge, and I kept hitting him. On and on, the coldness in me burning far more than any heat had ever done.

I felt Veronica's hand on my shoulder.

Far off I could hear the singing of the match day crowd getting closer. Soon the area would be swarming with fans and police.

Veronica took her hand off my shoulder.

"Take off," she said. "Gaurav and I need to talk a little business."

I looked down at Gav, his face swelling and his eyes wide with genuine fear, "You don't get to call me Gypo," I said. "Nobody fucking does."

I walked away, keeping my eyes fixed ahead of me. At the main entrance I passed a white transit van with another steroid freak leaning against the door. The door was open and waiting. I caught a glimpse of ropes inside.

I grasped the bottle with both hands to stop them from shaking and somehow made it safely to the front door of my house.

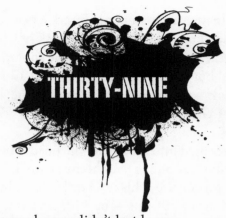

THIRTY-NINE

The silence in my house didn't last long.

As I leaned against my front door, waiting for my breathing to return to normal, the sounds of the football fans passed by behind me. Songs and chants, jokes and banter. It sounded like the Wolves had won the game. I didn't feel much like a winner.

The notebook was in my inside pocket. I pulled it out and stared at it for a moment. So much trouble for a few bits of paper.

Mary.

Bauser.

Janas.

My wife was mixed up somehow with Veronica Gaines. That would have been troubling enough even if I hadn't just sold myself out to Gaines too. I'd handed her Gav Mann, her biggest rival. I didn't want to think about what forced conversation they'd be having in the back of that truck or how it was going to affect the business. I'd sold out myself and my town, all to get out from under a rock.

Maybe I should have gone and joined the celebrations outside.

I decided to forget about it all. I threw the book on the floor along with my mobile phone and my keys. But something made me change my mind. I bent down to pick the book back up, and I noticed the stack of letters from Dr. Guthrie. I reached out and touched the top one and almost picked it up, but then pushed the thought away. I pocketed the notebook and turned back toward the kitchen with my bottle of whiskey. I felt movement behind me, but too late.

A fist slammed into the side of my head. My brain rocked against my skull. A punch caught me again, in the jaw. I fell, landing on top of the whiskey bottle. It hadn't broken on Gav Mann's head, but this time it did smash, turning into alcohol-coated shrapnel that sliced into me as I hit the floor. I squinted up, getting a look at my attacker.

Bobby.

He knelt in and punched me again in the face, then on the side of the head. He followed with rapid blows, angry blows. His face twisted into a snarl.

I ducked out of the way of his next punch and pulled myself to my feet. My side and stomach burned, and I saw the blood from the cuts I'd gotten from the bottle, thin trails of blood lacing across my clothes.

Bobby turned and stepped in for another attack, his fists swinging at me wildly.

"Not your stupid little helper," he said.

He directed his punches at my wounds, and each time he connected I felt another burn, the alcohol cutting through me. Each punch felt like it was driving glass deeper into me. The pain was different. It was colder. And as he pulled his hand back for a second's pause, I saw he was holding a blade covered in my blood. He was stabbing me.

I tried to hold myself up against the cupboard, my hand slick with my own blood, and he snarled at me again.

"Fucking sick of you talking down at me."

He drove the knife deep into my side, and I screamed.

Or I think I did. He twisted the blade before pulling it out, and he held me for a moment, whispering in my ear. Blood rushing in my ears, I couldn't make out what he said. It could have been a confession of his sins, or mine, or it could have been a knock-knock joke. He held me close as my body slipped into shock. He smiled and spat in my face before he let me fall.

The part of me that was conscious knew there was no reasoning with him. He dropped on top of me and stabbed me again. I didn't feel it. I was past feeling it.

Just stay here, I decided. *It's not so bad.*

I felt as if I would never need to move again.

My father's voice was in my head, insistent.

"If there's trouble, be far away from it. If you can't be far away from it, run like hell."

Get up.

I felt hands on my shoulders.

My father again. Pushing me. Making me move. Keeping me alive. I kicked Bobby hard in the knee, and he buckled awkwardly.

I rolled onto my front and pulled myself almost to my feet. I stumbled toward the hallway and almost made it before collapsing.

Bobby jumped on me again. This time I was facedown, and I felt a sharp, cold spike somewhere in my lower back. He must have stabbed me again. I was about to die. It came to me clearly, and it scared the hell out of me.

I remembered Bauser's dead body, his hoodie sodden with canal water, his body sliced open. Bobby's blade doing the work. The blade that was carving through me.

I remembered something else. I remembered Bobby standing behind me in my bedroom as I recovered my savings. I remembered putting the screwdriver in my coat pocket.

I felt inside my coat then, and my hand closed around the screwdriver.

Still there.

Bobby pressed down on top of me. I twisted round beneath him and brought my arm up, the screwdriver in my hand connecting with his face. I drove the sharp end underneath his chin, aiming for his neck. He tried to scream but only gurgled, falling back from my sight, from the tunnel vision that was closing around me. Somewhere my father was still shouting at me, demanding that I move.

Get up.

I tried to climb to my feet again, but couldn't.

Keep moving.

I crawled into the hallway. I dragged myself to where I'd dropped my phone. I dialed in the one number I could remember. Hearing my wife answer, I begged for help.

The static came in for me again, lifting me away from the world.

FORTY

At some point, I felt the world hit me.

It was like coming up for air in a swimming pool. The sound rushed to meet me from a distant rumble to clear voices. Terry Becker was sitting on the plastic chair next to my bed. It was a private room in the hospital, one of those rooms that smells vaguely of old people and is painted like a badly built Lego house. A clock was ticking somewhere, but I couldn't see one on the walls, so maybe I was imagining it. It's just one of the things you expect to hear in a quiet hospital. Maybe it's something to do with mortality. Snatches of other memories came back to me, of doctors shouting things, of people asking me questions, half-mumbled responses. I couldn't form them into anything solid.

"I'd ask how you feel," Becker said. "But I guess that would be stupid."

"Why change the habit of a lifetime?" I said with a weak smile.

It hurt. I made a note to keep my razor-sharp wit in check for my own safety.

"The doctors had to take something out. I think they told you?"

"Well, I do remember something that looked like a road-map inside a human body, and the guy pointing to the map seemed to think I should be paying attention."

"They did something to your intestines that I don't understand, except that they had to take a few things out. They say you'll need to lay off alcohol and spicy food. And you're going to be medicated up the wazoo. More drugs than Keith Richards."

"I love doctors." I smiled again and winced. "How long was I out of it?"

"All told, you've been pretty spacey for two weeks."

"Weeks? Christ."

"You scared us, mate. We thought you were going to die. For quite a while there, it looked like you would. Your mum's been having a nervous breakdown. This is the first time she's been away from your side in the two weeks."

I was quiet for a long time.

"Two weeks without a drink. My liver must think I'm dead."

He laughed a bit too hard.

"You need to take my statement?" I said eventually.

He shook his head but didn't answer. He stretched out his legs, his knees cracking, and scratched the back of his neck.

"Nah. Not yet. You've only just come round, and you're on too much medication. Wouldn't stand up in court. But we'll take it soon enough."

He was itching to say more. He looked like a five-year-old boy trying to keep a secret, his fingers twitching on his knees.

"What have you been told?" I gave him the in.

"Laura's filled me in on enough. We've made a hell of a case. Robson's DNA was all over a body we discovered in a flat off Junction Road. The knife he attacked you with can be matched to the one that killed Bauser. Then of course there's the fact that he hacked you a new asshole. Sorry."

I smiled. "It's OK. That was a good line. How did you find Janas's body?"

He hadn't told me the dead body was Thomasz Janas, but we both knew it was. I'd dropped that in deliberately, fishing to see how much he really knew and daring him to ask the questions that were eating at him. He stared at me for a moment.

"We got an anonymous tip about that one. But anyway, that's not the best of it. We also found Gaurav Mann, beaten to death in the same flat. There's enough evidence at the scene to prove Robson did him too. Not to mention a stash of drugs."

There had been no stash of drugs in that flat when I'd searched it. It was most likely the same stash of drugs that had vanished from Janas's possession the day he was arrested. I knew it, and Becker had to know it too. But he was too smart a man to say anything about it. And Gav, beaten to death. I felt a pang of guilt, but the medication killed it soon enough.

"It's all very neat and tidy from the sound of things."

Becker nodded.

"Looks like Laura's going to get the DCI desk permanently, and I may be stepping up to DI. Even that idiot Joe Murray, you remember him? Well, he's getting his reward for keeping his gob shut. He's a sergeant now."

I thought for a second before nodding. It all seemed like a lifetime ago.

"And am I under arrest?"

"Arrest? Of course not. You're a minor celebrity. Laura's gotten a lot of credit thrown at you. She says you worked with us to bring the case together."

"And Bobby's not claiming any different?"

Becker shrugged and refused to meet my eyes.

"Well, he's not in a position to say much of anything right now, because some guy shredded his tongue with a screwdriver." I winced, and he nodded. "But he's not arguing his case. Laura's worked on him and thinks she's about to break him into making a written statement."

"Where's my stuff?" I said.

Becker opened the cupboard next to my bed, showing me my clothes on a hanger and my possessions in a bag. I raised myself unsteadily to sit on the edge of the bed and went through the bag.

"Where's the notebook?"

Becker looked at me, and I could read in his eyes that he was being honest.

"That's all there was, Eoin. That's everything you had when you were admitted."

Becker stood. The plastic chair made a scraping noise as he pushed out of it. He brushed his trousers down for imaginary dust. I remembered something as he turned to leave. "What about your pensioner case?"

"She was too scared to identify the attacker. Some get sorted, some don't." He shrugged. "I'll let you get more rest. I can phone your mum and tell her you're back with us again. Oh, one more thing. There's this woman been asking to see you, but we're only allowing close family and police in."

"What's her name?"

"Rachel."

"I'd like to see her."

He nodded and left me alone with my thoughts and a phantom ticking clock.

Next time I opened my eyes, Rachel was perched on the edge of the bed, smiling at me. She had a backpack. She looked ready to travel.

"Where are you going?"

"Ireland. Mary still has family over there. I thought somebody should go and see them, as the police never will."

"What will you tell them?"

"I don't know, really. I was going to cross that bridge when I got to it."

"Fair enough. I guess really it should be me that tells them, but since you're volunteering for the job—"

She smiled again. It was better than a slap.

She put her hand on mine and squeezed gently.

"It was the right thing, what you did. You know that?"

"I've been trying not to think about it."

"I mean, it won't get you into heaven, but nothing does anymore. I just mean that bad things happened, and you were the one person who did something about it." She paused, as if waiting for me to argue, then continued. "I've been thinking about it. My whole 'you' project. Do you remember what you said to me, at my place?"

"That nothing matters?"

"Yes. You said we live in a world where nothing we do matters. Which is just about the most depressing thing anyone's ever said to me. And I go to AA meetings. Trust me when I say I've heard some depressing shite."

We both laughed at that.

"But that's the key, I think," she said. "Right there. You've been too self-absorbed to see it. You talked about the old man in the rain, about your marriage. You missed the point. The old man didn't die alone. He had someone watching over him."

"I didn't do a good job, though, did I?"

"What matters is what you did."

She smiled. It was almost the last time I saw it.

"That's it?"

"Yes. All that ever matters is what we do. And when you look at it like that, everything matters."

I shook my head but didn't say anything. I had music in my head for the first time since coming back to the world.

Deacon Blue, "Your Town."

Hamell on Trial, "Confess Me."

For the first time in a very long time, I felt alive.

She pulled a newspaper out of her bag and handed it to me and then set one of Dr. Guthrie's letters on the bed between us.

"Wolves are doing well, by the way. Thought you might be interested."

She kissed me on my forehead, touched my lips with her forefinger, and left.

I sat alone with my ghosts for a while.

Then I turned to the sports pages of the newspaper.

FORTY-ONE

Almost dying was easy compared to almost living.

I was given a long lecture by my doctor, a young Pakistani man with a serious face. Bobby's blade had fucked me up good. Part of my intestines had been removed and the hole spliced together like an electrical cable. The pain in my leg had something to do with muscles in my lower back, and along the way I'd tweaked my hamstring. The doctor said the limp might go in time.

The blood loss could have been enough to kill me. He told me that I was lucky Laura had got me to the hospital so fast and that the feeling of lethargy I was experiencing would last for a long time. He wanted to keep me in hospital for another three or four days, just to make sure I was improving.

I was prescribed what amounted to a medicine cabinet: drugs for my abdominal pain, drugs for my leg pain, water tablets to counteract the cheery side effects of a diet of painkillers.

The regulars at Posada chipped in to buy me a Chuck Ragan CD, with a note saying that it was exactly the kind of depressing male bollocks that I'd love. And they were right. Gaines sent me a card in which she again offered to hire me for the youth project. She said she was my new guardian angel, making all my problems go away. I hadn't realized the devil would be so good looking or the deal so easy to make.

On my last evening in the hospital, Laura finally visited.

"It's good to see you're OK," she said. "Dr. Bassi has been great. I'm sure he'll be by to go over it all with you again. Basically, Eoin, you've been very lucky."

There had been a pain building in my stomach for the past hour, and the pills didn't quite seem to be covering it.

"I feel lucky," I said.

Laura walked around the bed to stand looking out of the window. I realized I hadn't looked out the window yet.

"You'll need to coach me for my statement," I said. "Make sure I say all the things you want me to."

"Yes." She didn't turn to look at me.

Neither of us said anything for a while.

"You knew everything, didn't you? The whole thing: the drugs, Janas, Gav. You were going to play it all to get the promotion."

She laughed, and I didn't like it. It was a different laugh, harder and colder, than I'd heard from her before.

"It's best forgotten."

"And Bobby? Why isn't he trying to save himself?"

"He's not going to be doing much talking for a long time. He's doing a fair amount of clicking and grunting, but he's not talking so well."

I refused to feel guilty about that. The fucker had been killing me.

"But he can write, type, and blink his bloody eyes," I said. "So you got that statement."

She smiled. "Yes. I've taken a written statement from him, and it backs up everything yours will say." How had she gotten a statement out of Bobby that cleared me at his own expense? What was the leverage? What was really going on here? Laura must have read my thoughts, as only she and my mother could.

"He needs protection. He's going down for killing Gav Mann, and there's bound to be payback from Gav's big brother. He's too scared to cross me at this point."

I thought back to Veronica's card, her making all my problems go away. Things were leading in a direction I didn't want to go.

"Why are you protecting me, Laura?"

She opened her mouth, but no words came out at first. When they did, they were hushed and direct.

"Because I'm your wife."

"Where is the notebook? I had it when Bobby attacked me, but it never made it to the hospital. Where is it?"

"I don't know what you're talking about," she said.

She could lie to anyone in the world except me.

She blinked. Once. Twice. The message was there, unwritten. This was about more than promotion, more than her police career and the case of the century. She was dirtier than I had ever been.

"Was that the deal you made? You get the case, the press, and the promotion. Gaines gets the business? And what's next? You're knee-deep in it now. You'll never get out."

What a couple we made. She'd framed Bobby with one murder while I'd allowed him to get away with another. I'd handed Gav Mann over to Veronica Gaines to save my own skin and covered up Mary's murder along the way. Laura had sold out to the Gaines family, giving them a monopoly over the drugs trade. We were both in over our heads. There are lies, damned lies, and marriages.

I closed my eyes.

"Congratulations on the promotion," I said. "I want a divorce."

She mumbled something before she left.

I couldn't tell if it was "I love you" or "good-bye."

"Let's go and say a prayer for a boy
who couldn't run as fast as I could."

—Father Connolly

Acknowledgments

Pull up a chair.

Comfortable?

First thanks go out to the woman who made me into the man I am and who taught me never to sit down and shut up; thanks, Mum. And of course, I owe just as much to the woman who *keeps me* the man I am, my wife, Lisa-Marie.

I wouldn't be a writer if my two grandfathers hadn't made me into a storyteller, so for hours spent listening to them, talking to them, and trying to impress them, I owe Bill and Trevor. And for that matter, my grandmothers, who did everything else for us while we did all that. I owe my dad more than he'll ever know, for being the man he is and for setting an example for me to follow, and I owe my father for whatever that connection is that means we understand each other sometimes in ways others don't.

And my brother. I don't need a reason to thank him other than he's my brother.

Writing is a messed up and confusing road to walk by yourself. So I'm glad I've never had to. Allan Guthrie was the best Mr. Miyagi a young(ish) writer could have had. For taking a chance on me, for believing in this book, and for putting up with my insane e-mails, I owe way too many thanks to Stacia Decker.

For wise words, filthy jokes, and good suggestions, thanks go out to Ray Banks and Professor Steve Weddle. And for the best writer support network there is, thanks to all DSD'ers past, present, and honorary; Russel, Dave, McFet,

Joelle, Scott, Mike, Sandra, Brian, Bryon, JHJ, Chuck, Gerald, Dan, and the many readers who've made that site work. Thanks to Paul Montgomery and Dave Accampo, who aren't DSD'ers but feel like they should be.

Still there?

Good, some important ones left.

Huge thanks go to Franz Nicolay and Maria Sonevytsky, for being open to me borrowing their words. Thanks to Joe Murray and the man known as "Rozza" for putting up with fact-checking and my many strange questions.

And last but not least, the people who've actually made this thing into a book that's in your hands. Massive thanks to Andy B. for bringing me into the fold, to Jacque and Rory for helping me through the steps, and to both Kate C. and Renee J. for getting the book to stand on its own legs.

ABOUT THE AUTHOR

A Black Country native, Jay Stringer was raised on pulp fiction, comic books, morgue humor, music, and films. He found inspiration for *Old Gold* in his UK homeland and the postindustrial region where he grew up. Currently living in Glasgow, he has been published in *The Mammoth Book of Best British Crime*, volumes 8 and 9, and considers his works to be pieces of "social pulp." Alongside writing, Stringer has been a zookeeper, a bookseller, a video editor, and a call center lackey. *Old Gold* is his first novel.